Beautiful Dark

D1445144

Talisha L. Walton

TALISHA L. WALTON

DEDICATION

For the beautiful dark, Jocelyn Morris—God's light shines in the darkness.

ACKNOWLEDGEMENT

Jeremy Coutee, Keisha Winn, Keisha Benoit, Tavares Dixon, and Telvin Beauregard—please know that a day doesn't go by without me thinking of you. May our dad, Melvin Winn Jr., forever remain immortal in our hearts.

I Love You

In loving memory of...

Melvin Winn Jr.

April 12, 1961 - March 24, 2017

May your descendants increase greatly in number and be blessed—forevermore.

CONTENTS

Allen County Public Library
Saturday October 14 2017 02:17PM

Barcode: 31833071695271
Title: Beautiful dark
Type: BOOK
Due date: 11/4/2017,23:59

Total items checked out: 1

Telephone Renewal:(260)421-1240
Website Renewal: www.acpl.info

CONTENTS

PROLOGUE

"When an evil spirit leaves a person, it goes into the desert, searching for rest. But when it finds none, it says, 'I will return to the person I came from.' Then the spirit finds seven other spirits more evil than itself, and they all enter the person and live there. And so that person is worse off than before."

—Luke 11:24; 11:26 (NLT)

A stream of steamy hot water spilled over onto the floor as a bare dark-skinned damsel descended below.

Bubbles raced to the surface of the water in a seventy inch long, forty inch wide, and twenty inch deep cast iron freestanding vintage style bathtub that was chosen as first choice in a possible aquatic death.

The rushing bubbles were from the beautiful dark woman who had freely exhaled to release the oxygen from her chest, in an attempt to surrender—giving in completely to the invading floodwater that surrounded her.

An acoustic sound of running water echoed loudly underneath, drowning out her dark and endless thoughts —thoughts she'd do anything to forget, but for only a moment to regain the clarity and sanity she once had before.

The dark beauty was desperately praying for unconsciousness as she willingly yielded to a watery grave.

She was tired of being weighed down with disgrace— in disgust because the beauty was disrupted beyond disbelief, disturbed in her own despair and defeat.

The beautiful dark woman was discontent, disheartened, and deeply disappointed, and all she wanted in this darkest moment of all her days was to put an end to her dysfunction.

Her eyes fluttered in the deep as a distorted, but familiar, dark figure above her came into distinctness.

When the dark distorted demon realized she clearly recognized him, he flashed her a wicked grin.

Her eyes became ping-pong balls as his face became even clearer, causing her heart to sank into the pit of her stomach.

"Do you really believe this will work, stupid girl? You can't drown yourself in an old bathtub this way— especially alone. Now, Monica, if you'd like, it would be an honor to do you the favor of holding you down under until you stop kicking."

She gasped jumping to her feet as blood drew away from the surface of her skin, giving her naked flesh a grayish hue.

She quickly yanked a decorative floral towel from its hanging place near her in a quick attempt to cover herself.

Responding with chattering teeth and a shaky voice, she said, "What are you doing here, Erebus? Letitia ostracized you. You can't be here."

"Yeah, about that—I was here first. Are you and I back to being aloof? Drop that towel, Monica. It's not like I've never seen you naked before," he reminded her with grim hilarity.

"Since when have you ever called me by my real name, anyway? I thought you hated it. Call me by the name you gave me because of the feeling you get whenever my presence is near. I really miss hearing you say it."

"E-e-rie," Monica reluctantly responded with tear-filled eyes and choppy speech.

"Why are you here, Eerie? How are you even here right now? You're not even supposed to be here."

"But, I am here, my dearest dark damsel. I came back to be with you—my only love. Where is Letitia now, dark child? Did you think her weak and pathetic prayers would drive me away forever? How naïve," he teased.

"She rejected you didn't she? Rather insipid, Monica—you should've seen that coming."

"And, you're any better, Eerie? You don't love me. You don't really care about me. You lied to me and Letitia said—."

"Letitia said what?" Erebus angrily interrupted, "What did she say, dark and lovely, that demonic spirits are incapable of love? Surely, you don't believe every single word that comes out of that Jesus freak's mouth, do you? I do love you and that'll never cease from being so because you, my darkest sweet, Monica—belong to me."

Monica's bottom lip quivered as tears flowed freely down her dark flushed cheeks and drenched her face.

She whimpered and slid back down into the steaming hot bathwater as a spirit of suicide continued to tempt her, a spirit of fear shook her to her core, a spirit of despair swept over her, a spirit of sickness spread inside, a spirit of anger provoked her, a spirit of confusion clouded her mind, and a spirit of hopelessness invaded her heart.

Erebus, whose name means, deep darkness—a spirit of darkness, went back into his previous resting place to reside once again within the beautiful dark—Monica Dupree.

Bringing her knees up to her bare breast, she wrapped her arms around her legs and lowered her head on them.

Her entire body shook out of control as she sunk back into a well-known weariness of worthlessness.

Erebus cackled loudly and it echoed throughout Monica's bathroom, poured over into the hallway and then down the stairwell invading every room throughout the entire two thousand square foot wood-frame white house with a wraparound porch.

1...NO REST FOR THE WEARY

"Lord, see my anguish! My heart is broken and my soul despairs,

for I have rebelled against You. In the streets the sword kills,

and at home there is only death."

—Lamentations 1:20 (NLT)

In a cold dark bedroom, Monica laid still on her back in the center of her king-size bed.

She was wrapped tightly in a thick oversized black and white checkerboard blanket, staring up at a high ceiling above her.

She attempted to comply with the demands of drowsiness, but sleep was refusing to cooperate.

She even tried to play a relaxing game with rest, but it had declined to participate.

If only to partake in such a repose luxury would be nice, but the pleasure and indulgence of slumber, gave her the runaround.

All Monica wanted to do was sleep, but she was restless and being continuously harassed by a spirit of darkness.

"Monica, no one cares about you. You're worthless and pitiful," he taunted, pestering her with lies.

"Everyone despises you, run all over you, and hate to see you coming. You might as well end your pathetic little life. Go ahead and rid yourself the embarrassment of returning to college because they'll all know the truth about you once your little secret comes out."

"Please," Monica pleaded.

"Stop it. Leave me alone," she whispered through her weeping.

"Am I not the only one who has always stuck by you?" He asked.

"You've deceived me, lied and schemed against me, and exploited my abandonment issues for your own selfish reasons and personal gain," she responded.

"Who told you that? Was it that Jesus freak? You're not smart enough to figure that out on your own."

Monica began crying again as the spirit of confusion reared its ugly head, and brought up to the surface with it, the spirit of despair.

"Please now," she begged, "Just leave me alone."

"Now, you know I can't do that."

"Can't or won't, Eerie?"

"Does it even matter? I'm here to stay, Monica—my semisweet dark chocolate."

Monica shut her eyes, covered her ears with her hands, balled up into a fetal position, and started screaming.

Erebus caused a strong wind to blow out of control in her dark bedroom.

Dresser drawers flew open and clothing started ejecting out onto the floor and across the room.

He caused the wind to form a tornado, pulling into it items from throughout her bedroom.

Monica stood up in bed and yelled to the top of her lungs, "Stop it!"

Everything moving, ceased and fell to the floor as Erebus burst out into a wicked laughter.

Monica's vision grew dark and she collapsed onto the bed.

When she came to, she was no longer lying in bed, but instead, lying on her uncle's kitchen floor in the past.

Lying directly across from her was her favorite first cousin at the time, Amberlee Dupree.

Amberlee had the palm of her hand cupped under her chin.

Her long curly brown hair swept across the floor every time her other hand glided across a wooden antique board, along with one of Monica's hands.

"Where did y'all find this voodoo board?"

Kimberlee Dupree, Amberlee's twin sister, asked as she entered the room.

"It isn't a voodoo board, silly sister. It's a Ouija board. Monica and I are gonna summon her dead mother," Amberlee explained.

"Do you have to say it like that, Amber?" Monica asked frowning.

Amberlee looked up at Monica and apologized.

"It ain't gonna work, fools."

"Sure it will—cop-a-squat," Amberlee insisted.

Kimberlee tucked her light purple sundress under her bottom and took a seat on the floor next to her sister.

"First of all, it ain't gonna work because you two idiots are positioned wrong," Kimberlee informed them.

"How do you even know that?" Monica and Amberlee asked in unison.

"Um, because, I seen it on television. Now, follow my lead."

Monica and Amberlee did as Kimberlee asked by placing their fingers on the planchette and moving it around.

The teenage girls swayed back and forth on the spirit board moving in a figure eight, patiently waiting on something supernatural to happen.

Monica and Amberlee had been trying every weekend for weeks, with no success.

"I told y'all this stupid thing wouldn't work," Kimberlee remarked as she stood up to leave.

"Wait, Kim," Monica pleaded, "Don't leave. We haven't even tried calling out to her yet."

"Monica, I know how bad you want closure with your mom, but you and I have tried for weeks now, and nothing has happened," Amberlee leaned over and whispered, trying to reason with her.

Kimberlee turned around with her hands on her hips and walked back towards them.

"Ok, fine. I'll call her and you two dummies can just

keep that nonsense up."

Kimberlee looked up to the ceiling and began yelling, "Aunt Mona, get your big black butt down here immediately! Put that harp down, ditch the halo, and come down off those clouds—right now. Your ugly tar baby, Monica, wants a word with you!"

Amberlee's pale yellow cheeks became the color of blood as she looked up at her twin sister.

She looked over at her little cousin sympathetically and apologized sincerely with her eyes.

Monica got up and ran out the backdoor in tears, slamming the screen behind her.

"Kim, why on earth would you do that and say such an awful thing to our cousin? What if it was our mom who had died? How would you feel if she said that to us?"

Monica could hear Amberlee inside cutting into her twin sister for being mean and hurting her feelings with careless words.

Kimberlee smacked her lips and crossed her arms

before answering Amberlee's question.

"Monica is a dark dumb doofus. And, so what if it was our mom? She's dead to me anyway."

"Our mom is not dead, she left. See the subtlety in the distinction? You're unbelievable," Amberlee responded in disbelief.

Amberlee smacked her lips, rolled her eyes, and walked away from her terrible twin to join her crying cousin on their back porch.

"I'm so sorry, Mon'. You know how Kim is," she said in an attempt to comfort her as she placed an arm around her back.

"It's all good, and I'm good. I wouldn't expect anything less from Kim," Monica assured her.

Amberlee rested her head on Monica's shoulders and whispered softly, "I miss her too, cuz. Her death was senseless and she didn't deserve to go out like that."

"I just want to see her again. I'm not going to survive long without her."

"You will survive—one day at a time," Amberlee told her, "Just not this way."

"Maybe you can't reach people who have died and gone to heaven with a Ouija board. Maybe only lost souls can be contacted. Not being able to reach her, could be a good thing, Monica, and should be a comfort to you because it probably means she is at peace."

Monica smiled slightly, "Maybe you're right, Amber. Thank you, cousin."

"Of course, I am and no problem. That's what family is for," Amberlee said with a big cheerful smile.

"I'm gonna keep the board and take it home with me, though; if it's okay with you, Amber."

"It's fine with me, Monica. Now, it's yours—keep it."

Monica hugged her cousin.

She closed her eyes tightly and took a deep breath before opening them again.

Letting Amber go, she turned and leaned forward resting her arms on the vinyl railing of the back patio fence.

As Monica looked around her uncle's huge backyard, she noticed someone standing off in the distance watching them, with a wicked smirk, from behind a tree.

"It was you," Monica whispered in horror as she began to recover from her faint.

"Of course, it was," Erebus answered with the same wicked smirk.

"You called me, so I came."

"I didn't call you, Eerie. I was calling for my mom."

"Did you think she'd come? She hates you for causing her death. It was, surely, your fault she was killed and your dad hates you, too because he knows it—and you know it. Every time he sees your face, he remembers how much he hates you for taking his lovely sweetie away."

Monica covered her ears with her hands and started yelling, "Stop it! Please, stop talking!"

Erebus cackled and disappeared from sight.

The tears began flowing freely as Monica remembered

her mother and became overwhelmed with guilt.

"Mom, I wish you were here. I'm lost without you," she softly spoke in a broken voice.

"I wish I had died instead of you. If I never would've snuck out of the house to go to that stupid party with Amber and Kim, you'd still be alive."

Monica, no longer able to cope, jumped out of bed and ran to the bathroom.

Water still covered the floor and had soaked through the carpeted area outside the door, dripping through the floorboards and leaking from the ceiling downstairs.

She almost slipped as she swung open the medicine cabinet searching frantically for sleeping pills with an added pain reliever a doctor had prescribed to her grandfather, who had died from old age only months earlier.

"I'm joining you, mom. There's nothing left for me here. I've lost my only friend in the entire world who actually cared for me. I lost grandpa, I lost China, I lost

Jermaine, and I lost you. I have nothing else to lose."

Monica popped the top of the prescription bottle, tilted her head back, and poured the pills into her slightly opened mouth.

Turning on the faucet, she cupped her hands together to drink, swallowing over twenty prescription pills.

Monica placed the empty pill bottle back on the shelf in the medicine cabinet before returning to her bedroom.

She climbed back into bed, wrapped herself tightly in her comforter, buried her head into the pillow, and fell fast asleep.

2...DARKNESS SURROUNDS

"Let that day be turned to darkness.

Let it be lost even to God on high, and let no light shine on it."

—*Job 3:4 (NLT)*

"Monica, so did you ask them?" Amberlee asked from the receiving end of a powder pink cellphone as Monica was painting the final coat of black nail polish on her toenails.

Monica took a deep breath, and readjusted the phone between her shoulder and her ear before responding,

"Mom's trippin' and you already know how my dad is. He's gonna say no."

"Stop being such a scared baby and ask."

"How about you come over here and ask," Monica suggested with sarcasm.

"Well, just let me speak to my uncle Pete. He wouldn't dare say no to me. Besides the fact that I'm his favorite niece, he needs me to lead worship in the morning," Amberlee bragged.

"No, Amber. Asking him for that reason, isn't a good idea. You know how he feels about Saturday nights spilling over into Sunday mornings in the choir stand behind his pulpit. And, the choices he have between picking a favorite, are you and Kim. Picking you is a no-brainer."

"Ha ha," Amberlee responded, with a sarcastic laugh.

"Well, Monica, just wait until they go to bed and sneak out. Kim and I will pick you up around ten o'clock at the end of the block."

"Cool, sounds great," she agreed before ending the call.

Monica impatiently waited in her room.

Nervous and wired, she peeped outside her door about every other minute checking to see if the light was still on in her parents' bedroom.

Monica knew that once the light went off, she wouldn't have to worry about them during the night as they would be out, too, just like their bedroom light.

She checked her phone and noticed it was almost a quarter past nine.

Growing restless, she continuously paced back and forth.

Finally, after waiting twenty minutes, their room went dark, prompting her to finish getting dress.

She slipped on a high waist black jean skirt and a fuchsia strapless top that exposed most of her back.

She was sporting a shoulder length bob with a swoop bangs that covered most of her left eye, and the new hairdo was flawless, courting very well as a great companion to her very mature attire.

She was feeling herself this night and had every intention on having the time of her life with her cousins, well—as long as the dramatist, Kimberlee Dupree, didn't start one of her usual dramaturgic performances.

"If my dad saw me in this outfit, he'd condemn me straight to hell," she mumbled to herself with a conceited grin.

Being a preacher's kid, Monica always felt like she had to be more rebellious than most to prove her worthiness to her more popular twin cousins, who carried on ridiculously as they did whatever pleased them.

It was the underlying reason why Monica was going along with the idea to not ask her parents for permission to go to the party in the first place.

She wanted to give the impression that she didn't fear consequences and did whatever pleased her, just like her older cousins.

Her longing for the twins' approval was unending, and she always did whatever they asked of her, exactly the way they wanted her to do it.

Besides, she knew her parents would just say no, anyway, and it didn't matter that she'd be a freshman in high school come fall because they'd always view her as a kid.

With her dad being a pastor, most all things going on outside of the church were forbidden, but as long as she didn't get caught, she'd live her life wild and carefree, just like her cousins live theirs.

Monica locked the door to her bedroom, though—just in case.

She switched on her radio to a light tune to make it appear as if she's in bed listening to soft music and didn't feel like being bothered.

If one of her parents just so happen to get up out of bed to check on her or for any other reason, she knew if they discovered the bedroom door locked, they'd think she'd fallen asleep with the radio on and wouldn't bother risking waking her because of church service early the next morning.

She quickly went over to the mirror, applied the finishing touches to her makeup, and smiled at the dark-skinned teenage beauty staring back at her in the mirror.

Monica was only thirteen at the time, but thanks to her mother's beautiful thick and curvy genes she inherited, the dark and lovely beauty was already a total knockout —unlike her twin cousins who were seventeen and still hadn't reached their full physical potential.

Monica's physical maturity made her fit right in despite being much younger than them.

After sliding on her fuchsia strapped sandals with decorative black gem stones across the top, Monica grabbed her cellphone and purse, flipped off the light in her bedroom then slipped out of the window.

As soon as her feet touched the moonlit freshly mowed grass, the house vanished along with the entire neighborhood leaving only her, surrounded by the black of night.

"This isn't right," she mumbled as she was allowed to come to herself, "This isn't, at all, how this happened."

"Where am I?" Monica asked aloud to anyone who'd care enough to answer her, as she looked around dazed and totally confused.

At once, she heard a wicked laughter off in the distance, and knew, right away, that it was Erebus.

Monica could recognize his eerie and evil laughter coming from anywhere and since "pitch black" is his "métier," she knew he'd caused the darkness to surround her.

"Where are you, Eerie? This isn't funny," she yelled out into the darkness.

Erebus had taken control over Monica's mind and had caused her to fall into a deep sleep.

He was forcing her to not only revisit the past, but act it out, as well, without having any recollection that it wasn't really happening.

It was only mind games, and in her mind, at the time, it was happening for the first time.

"Please, I'm begging you—stop this, Eerie."

"It's only a caper, my sweet. But, indeed, your very own marathon of flashbacks—starring you. Come on now, and play your part. Let's see if you can change how it ends this time."

"Don't do this—please. I didn't really want to harm myself. I only wanted to be with my mother. Where is she? I only want to be with her. Please, let me be with her," Monica desperately pleaded with a tear-drenched face on her weakened knees.

Erebus stepped out of the dark, flashed Monica his familiar wicked grin, and then he stepped back into the dark again, out of sight.

The darkness began closing in all around and then inside her.

She found it difficult to breathe as the scenery

changed.

Erebus sent Monica back to the same night—now, at the party, standing next to her twin cousins and some of their older friends.

"Monica, don't you hear me talking to you? Did you even hear just a little bit of what I've just said? Are you okay? Planet earth, Monica. For God's sake, get it together," Amberlee demanded.

"Are you okay, cuz?" She asked again, but this time with sincere concern for her.

Monica didn't answer Amberlee, but only looked around in confusion with a sick sense of déjà vu.

"I hope dark and ugly isn't deaf and dumb—too," Kimberlee remarked as she crossed her arms and leaned back in a stainless steel barstool.

"Kim, please don't start," Amberlee asked nicely.

"Girl, shut up," Kimberlee angrily responded.

"I'm fine," Monica quickly mumbled hoping the drama would end before it began.

"You're lookin' good in that black skirt tonight, Monica," a guy complimented from behind Kimberlee as he chugged down a beer without taking his eyes off of Monica.

She looked up and smiled nervously as she quickly uttered, "Thanks."

Monica couldn't help noticing Kimberlee's face turning red as jealousy and fury arose within her.

"Do you remember me from church? I'm Jermaine," the fair skin, six foot tall high school jock with closely cropped curly hair announced.

Monica caught a glance of her crazy cousin staring loathly at her out the corner of her eyes.

Lord forbid she makes the mistake of giving Kimberlee a definite reason to ruin their night, so she chose not to respond by putting her head down and praying for someone, anyone, to change the subject.

Jermaine belonged to Kimberlee whether he knew it or not, and Monica knew not to cross her in any way concerning him.

They were only friends, but Kimberlee made it clear to them all that she wanted something more, but Jermaine showed very little interest in her; nevertheless, he was still off limits and Monica, along with Amberlee, clearly understood that.

Jermaine was being persistent in pursuing Monica, though, and Kimberlee was growing increasingly jealous by the second.

"I love this song," Jermaine yelled out.

"Would you like to dance, Monica?" he asked while grabbing her by the hand and proceeded on down to the dance floor without bothering to wait on her to respond.

Pulling her close to him and yelling over the music in his strong southern accent, he said, "Monica you're extremely pretty for a dark-skinned girl."

"Whatever that supposed to mean," Monica mumbled under her breath, while rolling her eyes and then scoffed as she pulled away from him.

Jermaine grabbed Monica's hands and pulled them together in his enabling her from pulling away.

"Now Monica, my love, I didn't mean it that way. I'm not trying to say that dark girls are ugly, and you are the exception to the rule because my momma is dark. I used to watch her with my dad growing up and how she lived her life with such grace and confidence. It made me decide way back then, that she's the type of woman I want when I grow up—a dark and graceful woman that reminds me of my momma," he passionately explained.

"But, not in a weird and creepy incestic type of way, though," he added and laughed.

"What about, Kim?

"What about her? I'm not interested in her."

"Well, she is very much, so interested in you," Monica revealed to him.

"Well, that's just too bad," he responded.

Monica's smile widened as she informed him, " 'Incestic' is not a real word, by the way."

"What?"

" 'Incestic'—it's not an actual word, but I totally get what you meant," Monica said laughing in hopes to avoid an awkward moment between them.

"I know that, love," he admitted, "I was just checking to see if you did," he responded with a smack and a smile.

"I'm dark, Jermaine, but I'm far from graceful," Monica assured him with a flirtatious smile.

Thinking about what he had said, though made her realize why he never showed any real interest in Kimberlee, but had instead—her.

"Let me be the judge of that," he leaned forward and whispered in Monica's ear causing her to melt inside.

As Monica came to the realization that she actually liked him and was notably attracted to him, as well, she pulled her hands out of his and wrapped them around his neck.

With an intense amorous look, Jermaine smiled, placed

his hands in the curve of Monica's lower back pulling her closer to him and kissed her softly behind her ear as they moved, synced in harmony with the rhythmic slow tempo coming from the DJ stand.

Jermaine was totally infatuated with Monica, and she knew it and liked it; she liked him and her eyes revealed it which is why she didn't pull away as he leaned in to kiss her.

All that mattered was that moment, a moment neither of them wanted to end.

As the music played, they held each other close and for a brief moment, the world didn't exist.

Jermaine had been watching Monica every Sunday as she sung from the choir stand, dreaming of this moment and now his dream had come true.

Monica was in his arms and he didn't have any intentions on letting go.

He cared for her.

It was never Kimberlee, but always Monica he wanted

and he wanted her to know that.

"I knew you'd be here with your cousins tonight, Monica. You three are always together, which is why I agreed to come to this lame party when Kim asked me to. I wanted to see you."

Monica's eyes grew as big and bright as two motion sensor LED security lights as she remembered her crazy cousin, Kimberlee.

She cut her eyes over in Kimberlee's direction and knew then, without a doubt, that the rage displayed heavily on her cousin's green with envy face was because of her, and her acts of betrayal towards the twin would have severe consequences.

Amberlee even, who actually cared dearly for Monica, had a look of disgust and deep disapproval on her face.

Everyone from their small community in Copperas Cove, Texas knew that crossing Amberlee Dupree would have unheard of consequences, but crossing her twisted twin, Kimberlee Dupree, would be a far greater mistake.

As the twisted one becomes sadistic towards her betraying cousin, she'll began to whip up schemes against Monica that could possibly cause the devil himself to admire her vengeful creativity.

3...REMNANTS OF THE DARK

"Let the darkness and utter gloom claim
that day for its own. Let a black cloud overshadow it,
and let the darkness terrify it."

—*Job 3:5 (NLT)*

"Eerie, please. Stop doing this to me. Forcing me to reenact the day I lost my mom, who loved me most, is a horrible thing. Why would you do such an evil so great? It only proves right of what I said before concerning you—you don't care about me."

Erebus burst out in an evil laughter as his dark

presence hovered over Monica.

"My bittersweet Monica, you commit suicide and you accuse me of doing a great evil? No one likes a hypocrite."

Monica, still on her knees in utter darkness began to weep inconsolably slumped over with her face in her hands.

"I only wanted to be with my mom," she confessed.

"I never meant to—."

"You never meant to what, Monica? You keep saying 'your mother' as if you've forgotten—she wasn't the only one who was killed that night."

Erebus drew closer to her and with a subtle wave of his right hand, he caused Monica to lose consciousness.

She had entered, once again, into the dreamlike state to live out a tragic past event as if it was the present, and all the while still unbeknownst to her, it was a delusive and devilish tactic to taunt and punish her.

"Get up, you ugly tar baby and stop kissing that

asphalt," Monica heard her cousin, Kimberlee say as pulsating pain filled her chest and a burning sensation dominated the side of her left cheek and ear.

Kimberlee had tripped her causing her to slip and fall to the dark pavement outside of a recreational building the locals would often rent out to throw extravagant get-togethers or wild late night parties.

On this night, it was a wild late night party, and a night that no one would in this small town will ever forget.

"I'm sorry, Kimberlee," Monica managed to reply as she tried getting up from the pavement.

Amberlee ran to Monica's side to help her up.

"Monica, that wasn't cool and neither was it smart to kiss a guy that you clearly had known Kim was interested in," she whispered as she squatted down next to Monica on the blacktop.

"It wasn't like that," Monica lied.

Amberlee frowned, "Who are you trying to fool, cousin? You're a liar. I saw you. It's definitely is, indeed, just like that and a really dumb move on your part. Kimberlee won't ever forgive you for this and neither will I. You've crossed the line."

"It was just a stupid kiss. It didn't mean anything to anybody," Monica lied again.

"Look at Kim's face, Mon'. Does it look like it didn't mean anything to anyone? Jermaine was her first."

Monica's heart was crushed as she looked over at Kimberlee and then scanned the crowd until she found Jermaine's face looking embarrassingly back at her.

"Her first what?" She turned back and asked Amberlee in tears.

"Clueless, cousin. What do you think?"

"I'm gonna kill you, somber strumpet, and every single soul who loves you," Kimberlee overly reacted and threatened.

"I'm so sorry, Kim," Monica sincerely apologized.

"Not as sorry as you're gonna be in a few minutes."

Jermaine broke through the spectating onlookers and

rushed to Monica's side next to Amberlee, and grabbed her by her arm as she stood up to dust off her ripped skirt and torn blouse.

"Get away from me, liar," Monica demanded through clinched teeth.

"But—"

"Save your breath, Jermaine. And, to think, you weren't interested in her, but it seems to be to me that you were interested in at least something she had," Monica shouted.

"At the least, let me explain, Monica."

"No need."

"Oh, and umm—I called my aunt Mona. She knows you snuck out of the house," Kimberlee revealed with a satisfied look.

Monica turned to her twin cousin, and her heart dropped as a car horn blared like a trumpet, startling her.

It was her mother, Ramona, and the look upon her face was one of complete embarrassment and great disappointment.

"Kim, you called, Monica's parents?" Amberlee surprisingly asked, as if she didn't see it coming.

"Believe that," Kimberlee answered as she adjusted the thin straps on her tight acid wash black jean mini dress.

"It'll teach that, black bimbo a thing or two about stealing my man," she continued.

"It's Kim, Amber. Of course, she ratted me out. Funny thing is, I really don't blame her this time. My betrayal wouldn't dare come without consequences," Monica admitted.

"Wait, Monica," Jermaine pleaded.

"Don't ever talk to me or say my name again, creep," Monica responded as she rushed towards her mom's white Jaguar, and got in on the passenger's side.

She slammed the door behind her, crossed her arms, and started pouting.

"How could you, Monica?" Her mother asked as she drove off.

"This is the very last time I'm covering for you. You're lucky I'm the one who picked up the phone this time and not your dad. I take up for you and your rebellious acts of defiance time and time again, and you and your careless actions make a fool of me every single time," Ramona continued fussing at Monica without taking in a breath.

Monica didn't respond, but only sat there with her arms crossed, still pouting.

"You're only thirteen, baby. You have no business being out all hours of the night with Kim and Amber. Patrick lets them run all over him because Faye abandoned them, but you're me and Peter's only child, and over my dead body will I let you run all over us, like they do him."

"I'm really sorry, mom," Monica looked over at her mom and mumbled with sincerity in tears.

"I'm a terrible daughter, but I promise you this time, it'll never happen again, so please don't hate me," she begged.

Ramona took a deep breath and smiled as she looked

over at her young and lost daughter.

"I don't hate you, baby. I'm not even mad, sweetheart. I just want you to do better. I don't want to see you throw your life away like this, is all."

"I promise I will from this day on," Monica sniffed and promised Ramona, and laid her face in the palm of her mother's free hand as she drove with the other.

A beeping sound interrupted the sweet and lovely moment, and Monica looked over at Ramona's dashboard.

"Really mom—no gas, again?" She asked laughing.

"You're the only one I know who would risk running out of gas by driving on the E until it beeps to alert the procrastinating driver that, in a second now, it's gonna be completely empty."

Ramona laughed as she took the next exit to get gas.

If only Monica had known that this laugh they shared would be the last one, she would've cherished it more.

As Ramona pulled into the gas station and parked at

the pump, she tried paying there without going inside the convenience store, but something was wrong.

The pump wouldn't work, and there was something off about the surroundings, and she could feel it.

Looking around, she noticed the station looked odd as there were a few cars parked, but no people in sight.

A gut feeling told her to get back inside her car and drive on to the next one, but she ignored it, made Monica stay in the car, and went inside the store to have a look around.

Immediately, she knew it was a bad idea as she approached the register.

An elderly man laid immotile on the floor behind the counter bleeding profusely from a chest wound.

Romona gasped as she noticed another man lying in a pool of blood at the far end corner of the counter.

She could hear footsteps from a pair of steel toe boots come to a halt behind her.

She began to shake as warm tears blurred her vision.

Ramona knew it was her end and all she could think about was Monica outside in the car, and she feared for her life—not her own.

As she turned to face the masked stranger behind her, a sawed off rifle went off in her face.

Monica jumped out of her skin when she heard the sound of a gun go off.

She looked in the direction of the convenience store, and through the glass frame door, she watched in horror as her mother's lifeless body—hit the floor.

Frightened to death, Monica quickly lowered her head to keep from being seen as a six foot killer turned his head in her direction, trying to peer through the tinted windows.

Easing out of her seatbelt, Monica slid down out of the passenger's seat and climbed to the backseat, hoping he'd think her mother was in the car alone.

Terrified, Monica got as low as she could as fast paced footsteps headed towards her.

She knew it was him—the man who had just taken her mother's life and was headed towards their car to take hers.

Monica shut her eyes as tight as she could and whimpered a prayer, pleading for The Savior to save her.

She could hear the sound of an approaching car, and still terrified, she feared for them as their car pulled up behind her mother's.

The gun went off two more times and the sound of glass hitting concrete, followed.

She heard the killer's footsteps shuffling, as he ran off to hide from sight.

Another vehicle was approaching.

Monica held her breath and covered her mouth horrified as she heard a familiar voice shouting.

"Sir, are you okay? Where are the two females who were in the car parked at the gas pump in front of you?" She heard Jermaine ask.

"I don't know. Call the police and an ambulance. My

wife and I have been shot," the man responded.

Monica heard a gut wrenching scream, as heavy footsteps rushed back in firing over six shots before a tall cold-hearted killer jumped into an old rusty Chevy truck and screeched off into the night.

Monica couldn't breathe; she couldn't move.

In a state of shock, she just laid there, in the backseat of her mother's Jaguar and didn't budge.

She knew Jermaine had only left the party early because she had and with her gone, he didn't have a reason to stay.

Monica heard the sound of sirens getting louder and louder, ringing in her ears as an ambulance arrived to the horrific crime scene.

Monica continued lying there—motionless and emotionless.

The traumatic experience had left her numb.

She knew everyone around her on this fateful night had lost their life, but hers had been spared and she didn't know why.

"Eerie, how could you?" Monica asked in disbelief as she realized that she was dealing with pure evil.

Monica also realized something else that she hadn't before.

Her life was spared for a cause she didn't know, and she had selfishly taken it, but now in deep sorrow, regretted it.

Everything grew even dimmer as darkness began to become the only thing she knew as it closed in all around her.

She was sitting in the center of the abyss.

Erebus had placed her there and had left her there to twinge with every passing moment.

He stood before her with seven other unclean spirits that had formed a periphery around her.

They were the same seven spirits that had attacked her only days before.

Monica shivered as she could not keep warm as the

darkness was freezing and she was beyond benumbed.

Her heart ached for her mother, and also Jermaine along with the other four people who were killed during a senseless robbery at a gas station.

Monica cried out in misery—for she was in deep distress, distraught and disoriented to say the least.

She cried out to God to save her—to send an avenger to fight and rescue her from darkness, fear, despair, anger, confusion, sickness, hopelessness, and her own suicide.

"What did you think would happen, stupid girl that you would get rapt up in The Spirit? God can't trust you. He has forsaken you because you've forsaken yourself," Erebus taunted with a wicked laugh.

"I'm so sorry, Lord," Monica began repenting through her tears.

"Please, save me," she pleaded.

Monica was grief-ravaged and crushed with guilt, but she still continued to cry out even more as the unclean spirits moved in on her, and the darkness continued its torment.

She could feel something happening on the inside of her that she couldn't explain.

Someone was intervening through prayer—an intercessory intervention was taking place somewhere on her behalf.

An extreme nausea came over Monica, and she began to vomit from one end and expelled all that remained from the other.

Although, the deadly effects of an apparent overdose had been completely expelled, her spirit still remained cast into the outer darkness.

The fervent prayer from an intercessor had been effective, but Erebus was unremitting, and letting Monica's soul and spirit go without a fight was out of the question.

4...A FLICKER OF LIGHT

"I could ask the darkness to hide me and the light around me to become

night—but even in darkness I cannot hide from You. To You the night shines

as bright as day. Darkness and light are the same to You."

—Psalm 139:11-12 (NLT)

"Do you always do what they tell you to?" Letitia asked

Monica regarding her twin cousins, Amberlee and

Kimberlee.

"I don't always do as they say. I have my own mind,

and I do whatever I please," she answered in an almost

convincing way, trying her hardest to convince Letitia she

was being truthful.

Letitia smirked and responded harshly, "Yeah right" as she laid back across her bed with her pen and journal.

It was freshman move-in day and Monica had made the mistake of giving a terrible first impression as she entered her and Letitia's dorm room for the first time, and in the very next moment, she wished, like crazy, she could take back every word she'd said to Letitia regarding her boyfriend, Adrian Grant.

Monica had stormed into the dorm room and told Letitia, that Adrian was still seeing her cousin, Amberlee, although he'd promised her that he wasn't.

Monica, then warned Letitia to keep an eye on Adrian because he's just another lying, cheating, and manipulating man, just like the rest of them, pitching the same old ridiculous saying that, "All men are dogs."

Monica tried convincing her that she's a fool for believing her man, Adrian was somehow different than any other two-timing loser.

Letitia's response to the accusations wasn't, at all, what anyone had expected, though, and she fed Monica's messy words back to her with a side of a few choice words of her own.

The year before, Amberlee and Kimberlee were seniors attending the modest college, Lubbock Christian University in Lubbock, Texas, and Letitia's boyfriend, Adrian was just another freshman attending the school, as well.

When Amberlee Dupree purposely ran into the tall, dark, and handsome freshman one day on the campus grounds, she was more than just smitten with him, to say the least.

Fully aware that Adrian had a childhood sweetheart, who would possibly be enrolling soon, from his hometown in Dallas, Amberlee still stopped at nothing to get at him.

After running up behind Adrian Grant for months, an opportunity presented itself for her to make a move, when Letitia Shriver failed to visit him on his birthday.

Amberlee ran on the opportunity to cheer him up after watching him wait for hours on his girlfriend to show up at the college.

"Don't look so downcast behind this girl, Adrian. You don't deserve to be treated like this. Let me take you out, and show you how they really do it here in, 'Hub City,' " Amberlee suggested to the depressed freshman on his b-day.

She suggested taking him out for dinner, then a few drinks, and possibly a little after hour entertainment if he was feeling up to it, but her plans came to an abrupt halt when Letitia caught them together and gave Amberlee a swift beatdown.

When Kimberlee found out about the mysterious bad girl who came to town and gave her twin sister a face makeover, she was furious, but Adrian's crazy girlfriend from Dallas, Texas was considered, by action and not saying, a whole new level of unruliness, and considered a hybrid of the common delinquent.

Kimberlee was much less average—extremely common in comparison and far from anything more villainous, she could think up in her simple scheming mind, than Letitia's worst.

The twins had been waiting on an opportunity to get even, and when they discovered that Letitia Shriver was not only enrolling in LCU, but would be also sharing a dorm room with their little cousin, Monica, they made plans to make her life miserable there.

Their well-built and structured caked-up plan came crumbling down as soon as Letitia tore into Monica in such a way that made her little childhood quarrels with, Kimberlee look insignificantly inferior.

Monica didn't expect such a hostile retort, but that's exactly what was given when Letitia's flesh-ripping words left her humbled and sorrowfully apologetic.

In actuality, Monica didn't really want to be involved in the, "Revenge of the Twins" vindictive plan and was so looking forward to meeting, Adrian's Letitia—the deeply disturbed and deranged Dallas dame who often goes by the name, Tia.

"I bet you're nothing more than their flunky," Letitia teased.

"You even look like one," she added laughing.

"Does your preaching pappy, who obviously has leadership skills, even know that you lack them?" Letitia asked as she kept right on browbeating Monica.

"Girl, you're a whole new breed of, 'Follower,' " Letitia teased as she sat up and crossed her arms.

Monica felt horrible about their senseless introduction, and Letitia knew it, but had given in to the anger she often struggled to control all her life.

Once she grabbed ahold to the cause of that anger, it became the ultimate challenge for her to pull back and release it, but God had done a significant amount of work in Letitia.

The struggle was getting easier, little by little, but not

this day.

"Honestly Letitia, my cousins made you out to be a really bad person which is the only reason why I agreed to say the things I said to you in the first place. If I'd known differently, about who you really are, I never would've came at you the way that I did."

"No, you're lying. You were hoping you'd be able to scare me with intimidating tactics and run back to your high-yellow mixed-breed cousins for cool points."

"That's not so, Letitia."

"Are you so sure, Monica?"

Letitia's anger subsided, and she put down her journal and got up from her bed to sit next to Monica on hers.

"Monica, you didn't even give yourself a chance to get to know me before you'd already made up in your mind what type of person I'd be based on what your messy cousins told you about me. Honestly, is that even fair?" Letitia asked in a soft spoken tone.

"Besides, Miss Dupree, I'm not that person anymore,

anyway. Had I been, this encounter wouldn't have ended well for you," she added with a harmless nudge in Monica's arm while giving her a warmhearted smile.

It peeked Monica's curiosity to know just what she meant by being a different person and Letitia was more than happy to share with her how Jesus Christ had recently changed her life.

Monica smiled at Letitia, with so much sincerity it lightened up their dorm, clearing the tension and negativity that had weighed the room down.

"Let's start over," Monica suggested.

"I'm, Monica Renée Dupree," she revealed still wearing the lovely smile.

Letitia returned a genuine smile and formally introduced herself.

"I'm, Letitia Ann Shriver, and you're surprisingly different and better looking than any other Dupree I've met. Are you sure they're your kinfolk? You all can't possibly be blood relatives," she teased.

Monica responded with a laugh.

She'd never met anyone like, Letitia who was so confident and sure of themselves.

Despite her cousins' corrupt intentions, the two of them had developed a really close relationship in the months that followed, and all was forgiven regarding their unpleasant first impression.

As Monica became aware of her dark surroundings again, the last words Letitia said to her were the ones echoing loudly in her head, not the prayers that she could vaguely hear her praying off somewhere in the distance, but nevertheless they were still taking the effect intended against Erebus and the stronghold he had her in, as well as the unclean spirits, accompanying him in keeping her oppressed.

"Looks like Letitia is at it again, and it sounds like she brought another Jesus freak with her," Erebus announced before his infamous wicked laugh that sounded a lot like two crows fighting, followed.

Letitia Shriver was, indeed, there at Monica's house and had brought with her, her best friend, another fervent prayer warrior, Desirée Baptiste, and both of them were interceding on Monica's behalf in a high-level of spiritual warfare.

Erebus knew he was losing, and he had no intent to go down willingly, but if he could deceive Monica into thinking she was losing too, he could trick her into helping him defeat herself.

"Letitia may have been successful in prayer and have prevented you from a fate of death, by suicide, but let's see how simple it'll be for her to release you from the demonic oppressions you keep hidden, and no one knows about," he taunted.

"Suppose she's just praying for you out of moral obligation because you can't possibly believe, my dark and sweet Monica, that Letitia actually cares about you," Erebus added as he continued trying to intimidate her.

"Especially, after what you did to her, with that whole

inappropriate move you made," he said as he burst out in laughter.

"Didn't you know, Monica that Christians hate homosexuals and preach to the world God does too?"

Monica covered her ears and screamed, "Please, Eerie. Stop talking! Stop telling lies!"

More laughter followed as a flicker of light sparked in the invading darkness.

It no longer mattered to Letitia what Monica had done.

She still continued praying for her, without ceasing.

It was mind boggling to Monica at first.

Erebus knew that, and was contemplating a conniving plan to use it against her.

In a quick and final attempt, Erebus tried forcing Monica to relive the last time she'd seen Letitia before Christmas break when the incident took place, and led up to the cause and prelude of many new sorrows, along with other unfortunate mishaps.

Monica knew she had crossed the line and even if Letitia did forgive her for what she'd done, their relationship would probably never be the same because of things concerning her Letitia knew about, but no one else did.

Erebus's attempt failed as it was intercepted, instead, by a different time, when Letitia helped Monica cast him out and drove him away the first time.

He had been manipulating her for years, and had deceived her into believing he was a good spirit—a spirit guide sent, by God from heaven to help lead and assist in helping her fulfill the purpose, in which God had created her for.

Letitia, having the gift of discerning of spirits, who could also see in the spirit realm as she has the seers anointing, and she revealed to Monica, Erebus's true identity, along with his origin and intentions.

One morning around three o'clock, Letitia had awakened to see Monica in the corner of their dorm room talking to a dark presence, that at first glance, Letitia excused what she saw as only a very dark corner because the room was dark.

The Holy Spirit quickened her spirit and urged her to opened her spiritual eyes, and look again.

God had exposed his true form to Letitia, prompting her to take immediate action against him, and that's exactly what she did.

Monica was dismayed for the next several days as The Lord called her to fast and pray with Letitia's help until she fully recovered from the whole ordeal.

The memory gave Monica the strength she needed to believe and have faith.

Monica couldn't stop crying and neither could she believe what was taking place on her behalf, but she was internally grateful and full of joy, that God was faithful and forgiving although she felt like she didn't deserve it.

She could hear, clearly now, what she thought at first to be a muffled sound of two females voices chanting, but she correctly perceived to be declarations in the name of Jesus.

It was definitely, Letitia there with her and another, demanding with boldness that Erebus release her and go back to the pit of hell where he came from, and was also instructing him to take his seven other demons with him.

Petitions and praises to God were taking place, as well.

It was all around her and she could literally see their prayers being answered as rays of light began to break through the darkness as the praying continued.

The spirits around her began to tremble with fear every time they heard the name, "Jesus."

They were searching around to see if He'd come.

Without a clear warning, they were all being yanked back one at a time as light invaded the darkness, and the light overcame them.

The Lord had given an order—a command that must and will be obeyed; a charge had been given, and Monica's life, yet again, would be spared.

5...INCONCEIVABLE FERVOR

"The Lord replied, 'I will make all my goodness pass before you,
and I will call out my name, Yahweh, before you. For I will show mercy to
anyone I choose, and I will show compassion to anyone I choose."

—Exodus 33:19 (NLT)

"The amount of passion you have is breathtaking," Monica mumbled to Desirée as she opened one of her eyes.

She had been listening to Desirée as she prayed in an unknown tongue for well over ten minutes without her even being aware that she had awakened.

Desirée was on her knees with her face to the ground on the side of Monica's bed.

Monica's muffled voice had interrupted her intercession, but she wasn't bothered by the interruption at all.

She opened her eyes and looked up at Monica providing the welcoming gesture of a caring and loving, warmhearted simper.

"Well, thank you," she simply replied.

"You're finally awake. How are you feeling, Monica?"

Groaning, Monica replied, "I feel like I've been struck by a thunderbolt."

Giggling, Desirée replied, "I see."

Monica sat up slowly to get a better look at Desirée.

"Wait a sec, I know you from school, don't I?"

With a smile, Desirée confirmed, "Yes, you do. I'm Tia's friend, Desirée Baptiste, but I mostly go by, 'Ré.' "

"I see," Monica responded with a smirk.

She couldn't help noticing Desirée's refined sense of

bearing and reposed sense of being.

Desirée has a supernatural gift to bear a burden for others so that she could effectively pray for them.

In carrying the burden, which would often come upon her without notice, she would intercede without ceasing until that burden lifted.

Truly an awesome gift from God, indeed, because within this gift, comes a calm that's hard to comprehend.

For in which we are called, we are also equipped.

Monica, also couldn't help noticing how beautiful she was.

To say that Desirée is merely basic in beauty would be an insult.

Average in height with curly short hair and a butterscotch complexion, her sparkling beauteous spirit gives her an illuminated appearance, and as a result, it causes her natural beauty to become aesthetic.

It is Desirée's passion for God that makes her magnetic, but that wasn't what had drawn Monica in or had caused peace to wash over her.

It was the alluring and affection of the Holy Spirit from within Desirée, giving off waves of tranquility.

Desirée got up off the floor and reached over to place her hands on Monica's temples, then began to massage them gently in a circular motion.

"That feels better, doesn't it?" She asked Monica with the knowledge of already knowing.

Monica eyes brightened, then she answered, "Actually, wow—it does."

"That thunderbolt you speak of is only a migraine," Desirée informed her grinning.

"It's from lack of food and the many tears you've cried. When was the last time you've actually eaten anything anyway, Monica?" She asked concerned.

"I know you probably expected more physical discomfort than just an awful headache after all you've been through, but 'Love' is—kind," Desirée told her with a tender loving smile.

Monica's heart began to break as her mind began to reflect back on the day before.

"Erebus, that eerie spirit of darkness, was right, Ré. God has forsaken me because I've forsaken myself."

Desirée stopped massaging Monica's temple and scooted closer to her until she was only inches away from her face.

"That unclean spirit is a liar. Just like the devil, he is. God is Love. He loves you, Monica, and there's nothing you can do about it, or do to change it. Take a good look at your surroundings right now. Does it look like He has forsaken you?"

Monica gave Desirée a halfhearted smile and halfheartedly agreed, "I guess you're right."

Looking around wondering, she asked, "Where's Letitia?"

Desirée cleared her throat and shifted her eyes downward to avoid making eye contact.

Not actually lying, she answered, "Tia went to the store

because you don't exactly have any real food in this house."

She couldn't tell Monica the whole truth that Letitia had been acting strange and didn't care to hang out in Monica's room while they waited on her to wake up.

Desirée didn't really know what had went on between them, or why they were no longer on speaking terms, but being a highly sensitive person with an empathic gifting, she could literally feel the disappointment Letitia had towards Monica, as well as the sadness and shame coming from Monica when she asked about Letitia.

Monica's heart was shattered because of it, and Desirée was having a hard time dealing with the heartache resonating from within her without knowing the reason why.

"Y'all's fallout was bad, wasn't it?" she asked breaking up the silence that was starting to descend in the bedroom.

Monica shook her head up and down with watery eyes.

"I can tell, but look on the bright side. Tia is here now, which means she still cares for you," Desirée said with much enthusiasm in hopes it would cheer Monica up a bit.

Desirée has known Letitia since they were in elementary school, and had it been two years ago, she wouldn't have even considered coming to see about Monica, let alone show any concern regarding her wellbeing.

She knew, though, that regardless of the circumstances involved in their broken friendship, the relationship they had established over the year, although broken, it wasn't severed so chances are they still had a chance to make amends.

"I pray you're right, because I know she's only here to keep the vow she made to pray for me over the next seven years."

"Oh my," Desirée expressed and giggled.

"Tia never told me about a vow. What vow?" Desirée

asked.

"And, why only seven years, Monica?"

Monica took in a deep breath and released it back slowly before giving Desirée an earful.

"The day we met didn't go well because I barged into the dorm room, accused Adrian Grant of being a cheater, and basically called Tia a naïve fool for allowing him to pull wool over her eyes. But, my gloating pride was taken when she lashed back at me with words that sliced into my flesh like razor blades."

"I'm not exaggerating," Monica clarified.

"She called me a wolf in sheep's clothing, and if there were any wool being pulled over her eyes, than I was the supplier."

Desirée exploded in laughter and after gaining her composure, she admitted, "I'm sorry, but that's funny and it definitely sounds just like her—turned down on low of course. She's usually a wildfire. I've known her since we were little girls. She has always been the master of put downs, and I can assure you, this incident only depicts her as a will-o'-the-wisp. It isn't even closely comparable to what she is truly capable of saying."

"Well, just wait a moment because I'm not even close to being finished, telling you about the, 'Ignis Fatuus,' " Monica wittily replied.

"First off, Tia called me a preacher's kid, who wears a lot of exceedingly long ugly dresses. Then, she said these exact words to me: 'I'm gonna pray for you tonight—that you, one day, truly find salvation and stop fooling yourself. Besides, it would be my pleasure to intercede on your behalf therefore consider me your intercessor for the next seven years, Monica Dupree, because that is typically how long it takes a cell to regenerate—since you insist on living in the flesh.' "

Monica concluded her story by reciting what was promised to her by Letitia, word from word. She even mocked her voice as she couldn't get it out of her head since that day anyway.

"Oh yeah, I almost forgot to mention this. She also named her vow to me—calling it, 'Fervor Favor.' Also, she hit me across the face with the Word of God," Monica added, as if it was an important and valuable detail that must be included.

Desirée bent over hollering in laughter as Monica frowned.

"Girl, that is beyond the funniest thing I've ever heard in my entire lifetime," she admitted.

"How in the heaven does one hit someone else across the face with the Word of God?" Desirée asked seriously wondering.

Monica continued to frown as she answered her question with her arms crossed, "It was with a Holy Bible she took out one of my suitcases," she mumbled.

Her last confession left Desirée undone.

She couldn't hold back the laughter as she fell to the floor tickled pink.

Monica shook her head and rolled her eyes at Desirée's

childishness.

"It's not even that funny, Ré," she said pouting.

"My God! Oh—yes it is," Desirée corrected still laughing.

Monica smacked her lips and continued pouting.

She had to admit that it was kind of funny saying it now, but not so much at the time it took place.

With that realization and all that had taken place, she really appreciated, not only the laughter, but the fact that she was capable of still causing someone to laugh.

She scoffed, then smirked and started laughing, as well.

"Oh, my God. I haven't laughed like this in so long," Desirée admitted as she sat up straight on the floor and looked up at Monica.

"Look at you, Monica—you're laughing too. God has brought you laughter," she exclaimed.

Monica didn't understand what Desirée meant.

"You're so beautiful, girl, with that tittering glow. Your entire countenance has changed, and your dark skin is radiant."

Desirée's praise towards Monica caused her to beam even more so.

"There's this verse in The Holy Bible, including the one you were hit with, Monica," she joked, "It's in the book of Genesis."

Desirée smiled at Monica as she began to tell her the story.

"After Sarah gave birth to Isaac, she exclaimed, 'God has brought me laughter, and everyone who hears about this will laugh with me.' No one, not even she knew that life would come out from her. So, think it not strange, Monica," she told her.

"God shall get the glory—regardless. You, like Sarah, was barren with no life in you, and it's considered shameful to a woman. It made her weary and she became disheartened because she couldn't produce life. But, God. He stepped in, and in all of her sadness and shame, she gave birth to Isaac, whose very name means, 'Laughter.' "

Desirée got back up again off the floor and sat in front of Monica on the bed.

She reached her hand out to touch the side of Monica's face brushing her straight coal black shoulder length hair back with her hand.

Desirée then proceeded to pour life into Monica with her words.

"Beautiful dark, Monica, as sure as The Lord lives, you will get through this. I know it's inconceivable in this moment, but mark my words and trust in God."

Monica began bawling and threw herself onto Desirée's lap.

Desirée comforted Monica by lying across her back and crying with her.

6...WHAT HAD HAPPENED

"Let them try to tell us what happened long ago so that

we may consider the evidence. Or let them tell us what the future holds,

so we can know what's going to happen."

—*Isaiah 41:22 5:16 (NLT)*

"There was this teacher once who told me that my bad attitude will be my undoing. What a nonbeliever, that guy. A supposedly good man—a teacher of little children who lacks faith in believing the children he teach, are incapable of changing. What's worst is he knows the gospel. When he had the chance to be helpful, he chose to be hurtful. If only he could see how wrong he was."

"He couldn't have possibly known, Tia. He was just speaking in ignorance," Monica responded with a smile as she leaned up against the wall with her arms crossed staring out the window admiring the beauty of downtown Dallas from Letitia's loft.

The topics of their conversations, since Monica had been there, were about encouragement, defying the odds, proving spectators wrong, overcoming disappointment, and most importantly, learning to forgive those who've wronged you.

Letitia had expressed to Monica how good it feels to prove those wrong who've said, "You'll never amount to anything," and she had a huge list of people who had said it to her.

However, success in proving them wrong can end up being an empty victory because now you're living your life as being so sure of yourself—hell-bent on proving everyone wrong about your worth, leaving yourself vulnerable to neglect caution.

Your overconfidence may weigh in the balance and become your own ruin.

In actuality, if you're truly confident in your ability to succeed in any and every thing you set your mind to, then chances are, you already know who you are, and furthermore Whose you are and therefore you're truly and fully aware that you have nothing to prove.

"I'm not so sure about that because knowing Christ, my teacher should've considered Him. It's no secret that Jesus is capable of making all things new. With God, all things are possible, so to modify the heart is nothing to Him. He can easily do that without breaking a sweat," Letitia said cheerfully with a joyous laugh.

Standing next to Monica, she crossed her arms and said with assurance, "Jesus is capable of doing the same thing for you too."

Monica licked her lips, lowered her head, and didn't bother responding because she knew and understood everything Letitia was trying to tell her.

She knew all these things concerning, "all things new" because her dad is a pastor of a mega church in Copperas Cove.

She'd seen over the years countless people get up, wrestle their way out of the pews, and take that faithful walk down the aisle to give their life to Christ.

It wasn't anything "new" about it to her, but coming from Letitia, she accepted it as so.

Monica had never met anyone like her, and her love for God was intriguing although she didn't understand it.

It was partially because of her upbringing.

Monica's father had always been strict, and her mother, too lenient which made it easy to play them against each other.

Every rule her father made, she made it her mission to break, and that's only because nothing she'd do good, was good enough in his eyes anyway.

He ruled his house with an iron "Bible," but if he had

to, sometimes he'd use his "fist."

The way Monica sees it, her dad is an imposter, not a pastor.

She didn't think her father, Pastor Peter Lee Dupree, was an imposter because he didn't keep the commandments, but because he preached from a spiritual book like he's spiritual, but didn't believe the spiritual things inside the book—rendering him powerless.

The change that take place through a relationship with Jesus Christ is spiritual and the making of all things new happens supernaturally.

He could cram as many rules from the bible down Monica's throat as he'd like, but it'll take more than words on a page coming from a powerless pastor to change Monica and set her free.

What had happened over the past eighteen hours, changed in her what the eighteen years prior, never could

As for the next eighteen hours that will follow however,

freedom shall certainly take place as The Lord steps in supernaturally, forgives Monica for her sins, and change her entire life forever.

First things first, though, Monica needed to clear the air by discussing with Letitia what happened between them back at the college that almost destroyed their friendship.

As Monica looked over at Letitia, she thought the best thing to do was just come right on out and lay it all out in the open so it could be addressed justifiably because there's definitely a back story to why it all happened in the first place.

Letitia beat her to the punch by asking an age old question.

"When did you first realize, you were gay, Monica?" She asked wearing deep concern on her face.

Monica wanted to come right out and tell her how much she hate men, but then Letitia would only as why and she wasn't ready to reveal a family skeleton that would send one person to jail and send others spiraling out of control, heartbroken, and devastated.

She really didn't want to be the cause of breaking up a family either even though they'd abandoned her years ago so Monica, instead, shared about the two-year secret relationship she had with her best friend.

"I can't really say when I first realized it because I simply don't remember," Monica lied.

"I guess if I had to say, though, I've always been this way. I had really strong feelings for a guy once, but he was murdered. A couple of years later, I got into a serous relationship with one of my closest friends who had always struggled with her sexuality," Monica revealed.

"Her name was China Yeung, but she went by the nickname, Chai. She was so beautiful, and I loved her so much," Monica admitted.

"Even now, I can't get the image of her beauty and elegance out of my mind. She wasn't named China just because her parents liked the name. Her ethnicity was

Asian and African American. China looked like her father with beautiful slanted dark brown eyes, but she had her mother's beautiful copper complexion and soft features," Monica said in admiration.

"See, what had happened was, I thought I didn't care who knew that we were more than just close friends, but when it came time to come out openly about our relationship, I chickened out and China turned on me,"

"Why didn't you just come out?" Letitia asked.

"My Christian family would've had a fit if they knew about us, also my mom had already died and sorrow was still hanging over our house. My dad remarried, but he still wears the wedding ring my mom slipped on his finger twenty years ago to this day like he's still married to her, " Monica explained.

"So, what happen between you and Chai?" Letitia asked and urged her to reveal.

Monica struggled to find the right words to expound on as her thoughts ventured off to the last words spoken between her and China Yeung.

"I don't understand why it's such a big deal! It's nothing to be ashamed of and I'm tired of living a secret lifestyle. It's no different than living a lie," China admitted so well beyond frustration.

She was furious with Monica for not openly sharing the truth about their obscured relationship.

China was certain about what she was and what she wanted, while on the other hand, Monica had doubts and feared consequences she would have to face at the hand of her father.

China knew why, but Monica wouldn't come out and admit it.

"I'm done hiding, Monica, my love, I was born this way, but you was made this way," China reminded Monica.

"Please understand why I can't do it, Chai," Monica pleaded.

China shook her head as she realized Monica never

had any intentions on ever coming out and admitting the truth about her sexual preference.

"Huh, so I'm the fool who's in this alone, right?" China asked Monica no longer able to hold back tears.

"I can't," Monica mumbled.

"Your stepbrother surely did a number on you."

"It's not about him," Monica quickly responded praying she could convince China to believe her.

China got up from her sofa and stood in front of Monica so she could look her in the eyes.

"Am I not right, Monica? You hate men and you're only with me because of what Dominique did to you, and not because you were born this way. You're with me because you're scared to be overpowered again by another man you allow in your life."

Monica fought back tears of guilt and shame.

She didn't deny it, but she didn't admit it either.

China didn't need her to come out and say it anymore, Monica's lack of a response was enough to convince her.

China shook her head in tears as she backed away from her.

"Please leave, Monica," China angrily uttered as she pointed towards her front door.

"Chai—don't do this," Monica pleaded.

China gritted her teeth and pushed Monica back towards the front door.

"Get out! Get out! Get—out!"

China kept yelling until Monica agreed to leave.

She ran out of the house slamming the door behind her.

She could still hear China sobbing inside as she slid down the side of her sand-lime brick two-story house, and did the same.

"Monica," Letitia called out.

"What?" Monica responded as she exited her memories.

"Are you gonna tell me what happened between you and China or what?"

"Yeah, of course. China ended up telling her parents she was gay, and let just say they didn't take it well."

Monica continued to fight back tears, and then cleared her throat.

"A few months later, Chai killed herself."

Letitia closed her eyes and a tear escaped down her cheek as her heart broke for Monica.

"I'm so sorry that happened to you," she sympathized and wrapped her arms around her.

Monica took in a deep breath, and said in relief, "good thing I didn't tell my dad," and tried smiling through her tears.

Letitia sighed and shared a warmhearted smile.

Monica looked back up at her with worry in her eyes.

"Are you sure you haven't ever slipped up and told anyone about me or what happened between us, Tia?"

"Girl, I slammed your face into the ground so we're even, and like I already told you once before, your secrets aren't mine to tell," Letitia reminded her.

"I'm really sorry I came on to you, though, Tia."

"You don't have to keep apologizing about it, Monica, because you and I—we're good. All is forgiven. I don't support or agree with your lifestyle, but I will never condemn you, bash you, or cut you out of my life for it," Letitia assured her.

"Thanks so much, Tia. I really needed to hear that."

"There's something else you need to hear too, Monica. Well, it's more so like something you need to know," Letitia clarified.

"And, what's that?" Monica asked as Letitia now had her full attention.

"Homosexuality is a spirit—a homosexual spirit. It's a spirit of perversion. However, it may be controversial, but I'm telling you the truth about what I see in the spirit. When it comes to discerning a spirit, I'm almost never wrong."

Monica just couldn't accept what Letitia was saying.

"That sounds ridiculous," she said and began laughing.

"Fine, don't believe me, then, but I'm telling you—it's so."

"How so? Please explain," Monica asked.

"The unclean spirit enters through a portal that opens as a sexual sin is taking place, and it attaches itself to the victim of the assault. Once a spirit attaches, it's easily transferred from person to person during sexual intercourse. Once in, the demon can play around like a chimpanzee, swinging from a family tree, choosing whichever branch it wants to rest on. And, this is why you hear so many homosexuals say, 'I was born this way.' "

"That's absurd! You're lying," Monica accused.

"Come on now, why would I lie about this?"

"That's what I would like to know!"

"Monica, seriously? So, you mean to tell me, that you believe in the transference of sexually transmitted diseases, but not the transference of sexually transmitted demons? You even know for yourself that you can inherit your mother's dark skin tone, her keen intelligence, and bad attitude, and also, your father's cocoa brown eyes, his witty sense of humor, and laziness. The good and the bad is handed down to descendants. So why then can't you believe me when I tell you that you can inherit their unclean spirits too? Because, these aren't habits of theirs you just so happen to pick up on, but demons of theirs that just so happen to pick up on you."

"I honestly don't know how to even respond to what you're telling me," she truthfully admitted.

But, she had to admit she wanted Letitia to be right because if so, like any other spirit, it too can be cast out.

With a sullen look, Monica wondered and asked Letitia, "Why are you telling me all of this for?"

Letitia smiled and tilted her head a bit.

"Monica, I am telling you this because you need to know that I will never, under any circumstances, stop praying for you, and indeed, God will deliver you and forgive you for all of your transgressions."

7...PRELUDE TO A PLUNDER

"The enemy boasted, 'I will chase them and catch up with them.
I will plunder them and consume them. I will flash my sword;
my powerful hand will destroy them.' "

—Exodus 5:19 (NLT)

"Didn't you know, Monica that Christians hate homosexuals and preach to the world God does too?" Monica heard Erebus say.

Hearing his voice was only her imagination and she was having the hardest time casting it down.

Anxiety was her pillow as she laid on her back in

Letitia's study on an air mattress looking around the room for sleep.

She couldn't get the words that Erebus had spoken to stop speaking in her ear.

Then, there were the words Letitia had just spoken earlier tapping her on the shoulder desperately wanting a chance to be taken into consideration.

A sermon her father preached once came into remembrance about the types of people who will not inherit the Kingdom of God and surely so, homosexuals are clearly stated as one of them; for in the Word of God, homosexuality is one of the sexual sins included in the first letter Paul, an apostle of Christ Jesus, wrote to the Corinthian church.

Monica's dad may not practice the supernatural parts of the Holy Bible, assuming as if it could be set apart, but he wholly put into practice the laws and traditions.

Now, thinking on it all, her mind quickly went back to the reason her sexuality is so perverted in the first place.

Monica hated men because of Dominique François, and what he had done to her that has ruined everything for every man after him who had come, or who would come, into her life.

Monica had turned her back to the very day her father brought him and his mother through their front door and hasn't turned back around since.

Her father's voice echoed loudly in her mind as her thoughts went back to that heavily despised day.

"Monica, dear? Come out of the kitchen. There's some folks I'd love for you to meet," Monica's father, Pastor Peter Lee Dupree, yelled as he entered the house.

Monica rushed out of the kitchen smiling from ear to ear to see who was visiting them.

Her smile quickly faded as she came face to face with a vicious hag and her demented offspring.

"Pamela and Dominique, this is my daughter, Monica. Monica, this is your new stepbrother, Dominique and your beautiful new stepmother, Pamela," he formerly introduced.

"Nice to finally meet you, Monica, We've heard so much about you that we feel like we already know you. The way Peter has been going on and on about your liveliness and loveliness, I'm sure we'll be a happy family here," Pamela cheerfully predicted as Dominique stared.

Monica didn't really know what to say; she was outraged.

She stood still in one spot with her mouth ajar as she stared too, but in transparent anger and conspicuous enmity.

"Aren't you going to say anything, dear?" Her dad asked as he pretended to be shocked by her rudeness.

"Or, maybe your plan is to continue looking daggers at us like that?" he added

"The ladder, daddy! You stay gone for two whole days then come back home with a new wife and her son expecting me to just set two more placings at the dinner table, and add two more dinner rolls in the oven so we all

95

can take our seats like a happy new family, say grace, and chow down? Are you kidding me?!" Monica angrily remarked.

"You didn't even give me the courtesy of asking how I would feel about you getting remarried which would've been only right since your last wife just so happened to be my deceased mother. Good to see that there wasn't anything unique about my mom—dark-skinned women are just your type," she stated and scoffed.

"I'm in love with, Pamela and have embraced her son as my own. They are going to be a part of this family, Monica, whether you like it are not. And, considering the fact that I'm a grown man and this is my house, I don't need permission or approval to do anything," Pastor Dupree expressed with extreme passion.

"Furthermore, I don't have to explain myself to you," he added.

"Whatever," Monica snapped back as she walked off.

"I'm not calling her momma—that's for sure," she

yelled as she headed back into the kitchen slamming cabinet doors.

Pastor Dupree, headed in after his daughter, caught her by the arm, and yanked her around to face him.

"Would you really be so rude, Monica? Would you continue to act so immature about this?" He asked a little less agitated.

Snatching away, Monica accused, "You're the one who's trying to replace my mom, not me!"

"We've already discussed this, sweetheart and we both agreed that it's time to move on."

"No, dad. You decided it was time. There was never any agreement," Monica quickly responded with her face covered in tears.

"My mom just died a day ago and you've already gotten a new replacement part like she was just an old raggedy detachable piece off your equipment that stopped working."

"Your mom—. No, my wife died a year ago and it isn't

meant for us to just die too, Monica. Life has to go on for the rest of us. You're not a child anymore. You know all of this."

"To me, Peter, it was yesterday and I'll never—ever accept it as being yesteryear," Monica clarified through clenched teeth.

"So, now I'm just Peter to you? Don't you think you're being just a little too dramatic, daughter? Perhaps, you've forgotten that my wife was alive and kicking before she jumped out of bed in the middle of the night to pick your bratty behind up when you were supposed to have been asleep in the bedroom down the hall from us," he blurted out without thinking first.

Pastor Dupree's face resembled an owl's face as he realized how much he wished he hadn't said what was now too late to take back.

Monica stood in silence startled to hear the words she already thought her father was thinking, but had never uttered.

She now knows for certain, though that her father does, indeed, blame her for her mother's death.

It was finally out—Pastor Peter Dupree thinks it's his daughter's fault his wife was killed.

"Sweetheart, I didn't mean what I said," he tried explaining, but it was too late to apologize because the damage was done.

Monica could barely catch her breath as she choked back a huge jar of tears.

She couldn't find an appropriate response that would be befitting to help in such an unbeatable situation, so she walked away in silence.

She quietly went into her bedroom, closed the door, and locked it behind her.

Unable to hold herself together, she collapsed on the bed, smothered her face into the covers, and wept— bitterly.

"Oh God," she whispered as she rolled over on the air mattress to one side and placed her arm under her head.

She thought about how miserable her life had been since the moment she met Pamela and her sinister son.

Dominique has lustfully watched every single move Monica has made around the house since the day they arrived.

He made her feel like a savory dish locked in a room with a hungry dog on a chain, and Dominique was that dog who couldn't get to the savory dish because he was chained to the wall on the other side of the room.

One day, someone allowed that dog to roam free around the room for an entire weekend, but didn't bother protecting the dish that would surely become a meal to satisfy the appetite of a dog that was no longer hungry, but starving.

"We've decided to take a cruise for our anniversary this weekend so I need you to keep a close eye on Monica until we get back. Can you be the grown up and do that for me?" Monica heard her father say to Dominique in the living room as she eavesdrop on their conversation.

"Of course. No problem, dad," he answered with enthusiasm.

Monica's heart shattered like glass in her chest as tears filled the corners of her eyes.

She gasped knowing the situation was bad and would get worse if left alone with Dominique.

She wouldn't last the rest of the night let alone the entire weekend without him trying to make a move on her.

Monica ran to her room to think of a plan to get away from the house for the weekend, as well; with Amberlee and Kimberlee away at college, she couldn't spend the weekend with them.

"Eerie," she whispered and immediately, he appeared before her.

"My dad and his succubus are leaving for the weekend. What am I going to do about the dog in heat?" she asked him searching his dark eyes waiting for a solution.

"Monica, that boy is harmless—believe me.

Dominique may ogle you with lustful eyes, but he wouldn't dare try to make an actual move on you," Erebus assured.

"Be not afraid, dear. You're safe here and I'll be here with you. Now, have I ever steered you wrong?"

Monica smiled and felt reassured because she trusted Erebus so therefore when her father came into her bedroom to share his good news, she had no worries and wished him a safe trip.

Pastor Dupree had left them cash and the fridge was already filled with food; they were all good for the entire weekend.

Monica decided to stay in her room to avoid Dominique as much as possible—if possible.

It was late Friday evening and she had high hopes she could get through two nights with the hound dog.

After sneaking into the kitchen undetected, the plan was simple.

She would quickly, but quietly prepare a sandwich,

grab a bag of chips and a coke, then haul donkey back to her bedroom to count one night down.

Monica knew that as long as she could hear the video game actively being played in the living room, there was still time for her to get everything needed before sneaking back out of the kitchen.

As she returned the condiments to the refrigerator, the game stopped and her heart dropped.

Her eyes shut when the fridge shut because she knew it was the dog in heat who'd closed it and was now sniffing at her coattail.

"Monica, why are you so tensed, baby?" Dominique asked causing her to cringe at the sound of his raspy voice.

She thought about making a run for it, but it was as if he had telepathy the way he quickly reacted to just the thought of her next move, by setting up a perimeter with a firm arm block trapping her between him and a hard place.

"Your darkness, how would you like to make an heir?" he seductively asked with a smirk.

"But, I'm sure the pleasure would be all mine, my queen, because you're looking hot and mighty to me in that royal nightgown," he told her as he tried looking down her top.

"Leave my presence and avert your eyes, peasant— before I have them smashed deeply within your skull," she wittingly threatened with a clever comeback.

"Whoa now, and that is why I love you, Monica, because you're a lovely one, who keeps all things interesting," he complimented as he released her from his trap.

"Thanks, lovely one," he whispered and kissed her cheek, snatching her cold cut sandwich, chips, and soda before exiting.

Her heart ascended again as he left the kitchen, flopped down on the sofa with her food, and grabbed the joystick to resume playing his game.

Monica was unnerved and no longer interested in food, though, as she quickly ran back into her bedroom and closed the door.

"Eerie," she whispered and he appeared before her again.

"I just had a close encounter with, Quick Draw McGraw's dog, Snuffles, and he wouldn't close his mouth until I tossed in a doggy biscuit," she said snickering.

"My clever girl, see now? I told you everything would be fine."

Erebus stuck around until Monica fell asleep, but before leaving, he veiled himself and roamed into the living room where Dominique had fallen asleep on the sofa.

For a quick thrill, Erebus commanded another unclean spirit to tempt Dominique into making a move on Monica.

"I wonder if Monica's asleep yet. She was looking so fine in her sleep-tee tonight," the spirit of lust whispered in Dominique's ear, to trick him into believing the thoughts were actually his own.

To do so, wasn't a hard task as all the evil spirit had to do was play on the feelings he already had for her.

"I can tell she wants me. Why else would she parade through this house all the time in too little dresses, if not to entice me? She wants me," the lustful spirit included as Dominique gave in to the temptation and headed down the hallway to Monica's bedroom.

Standing in the doorway filled with lust, he watched for awhile as she slept on her stomach with the covers pulled up to her waist.

He admired her beauty and the way her shoulder length hair wrapped under her chin as her head rested on a pillow.

Dominique sneered as her back moved up and down as she breathed in and out, but as his eyes followed down the curve of Monica's back, the allure grew hypnotic and swiftly overtook him.

He could no longer resist the urge to be near her as he gently eased into Monica's queen-sized bed behind her.

"You and I are destined to be together, lovely one. The moon shines from your window on us revealing our skin tones are precise when I pressed my body up against yours. For a moment it looked as though we were one," he whispered in her ear, "so, I pretended, for an hour, that you and I had fallen into each other."

Monica's eyes shot wide open as her stepbrother's raspy voice reached her ears.

He started breathing heavily on the back of her neck as the heat from his breath traveled down her spine.

Her voice trembled, "Dominique, please—don't," she whispered as tears escaped her eyes and soaked through her pillowcase.

"Come on now—just once," he begged.

"Be still, lovely one," he insisted as he wrapped his hand around her waist and then inside her nightgown.

"I—I am a virgin," she revealed trembling.

Dominique continued breathing heavily down her back while he held her closer, and softly kissed her shoulder before letting her go.

"And—I am in love with you," he revealed shamefully.

Monica's pillow was soaked with teardrops, but she still continued lying there trembling uncontrollably as the sound of Dominique's bare feet softly slapped against the hardwood floor and slowly faded outside her bedroom door.

8...HEART AS A ROCK

" 'Does not my word burn like a fire?' says the Lord.
'Is it not like a mighty hammer that smashes a rock to pieces?' "

—Jeremiah 23:29 (NLT)

A tall black middle aged man with salt and pepper closely trimmed hair and a well-groomed goatee that matched, fumbled around on his bedroom floor to grab his ringing cellphone.

"Hello," he mumbled in a husky tone as he cleared his throat.

"Uncle Patrick," Monica managed to say from the other end of the connection.

"Hey, pumpkin," he responded as he recognized her voice, sat up in bed, and looked over at his nightstand.

"What's the matter, Monica? It's five o'clock in the morning. What's going on?"

There was silence on the other end as Patrick waited on his niece to respond to his concern for her.

"Pumpkin, are you still there?"

Monica fought back tears before answering, "Yeah, Uncle Pat. I'm still here."

"You have me all worried about you now. Tell me what's wrong?" Patrick asked Monica again.

"Are you sure that there isn't a problem with you?"

"There's no problem. I just wanted to know if I can come over to your house to stay until my dad and his wife return home from their weekend cruise."

"You know that you're always welcomed over here, but Amber and Kim didn't come home for the weekend so you'll be here alone," Patrick explained.

"That's fine. Can you please come and pick me up tonight when you leave the farm?"

"Sure thing, pumpkin, but are you sure you're okay? Because, you got me kind of worried over here," he admitted.

"I'm sure. Just promise me you won't get too busy and forget."

"Okay, I promise, but I believe it would be a better idea if you call me around eight tonight and remind me—just in case."

"Of course," she responded before ending the call.

Monica threw her head back as she sat against the wall in the corner of her room thinking about what happened overnight.

She was still trembling, terrified about what Dominique might do if she stayed another night alone with him and cringed at the thought of his touch.

"Dominique is a psychopath and I got to get away

from this house before nightfall or I fall asleep," Monica whispered to herself.

"What do you think people would say about you if they knew that you sit in the corner of your bedroom talking to yourself?" Erebus asked Monica as he manifested before her.

Monica, still all shook up, jumped as he entered her bedroom.

"Don't do that, Eerie. You scared the bejesus out of me," she exclaimed.

"Oh come now, Monica, What's gotten you all spooked?"

Monica started crying as she told Erebus everything that had happened between her and Dominique.

"I'm sorry, Monica that I wasn't here," he lied, "I had to leave."

"You don't have to explain. I know how spiritual matters work," she said as she pulled up one leg to rest her chin on her knee.

"Monica, if I had a choice, I'd never leave you and would always be here to protect you," he lied again.

"I know," Monica mumbled.

"But, everything worked out just fine, right? Dominique is still stupid and you're still standing," he said grinning to cheer her up.

Monica attempted to smile, but turned her head instead.

Erebus moved closer and settled down low before her.

"I won't be able to be here tonight with you. Monica."

"That's okay because I won't be staying here with, Psycho tonight anyway," she revealed to him.

Erebus looked puzzled, "What do you mean?" he asked.

"My uncle Patrick is coming to get me as soon as he leaves his farm tonight."

Erebus had been scheming up a plan against Monica for several months and tonight was the night he had every intentions of following through with that plan, but he had to get her to stay home with Dominique in order for his plan for oppression to work.

"Don't tell me you're scared of Dominique, Monica. There's no way he could ever harm you," he tried convincing her.

"He doesn't scare me," she lied.

"Besides, it's not about being scared anyway. Dominique is an iron man and can easily overpower me if he wanted to without even straining a muscle even if I fought him back with all my might. Last night was, literally, a wakeup call, and that is why I'm going to my uncle's house," she justified.

Erebus gave her a sly smile.

"Get a nap in, Beauty. You look like you haven't slept, ever."

"I haven't because I didn't want to wake up and he's in bed with me again," she whispered with her head down.

"You'll be fine. Get some shut eye and I'll check up on you later," he said before vanishing from sight.

Monica had indeed lied, of course she was terrified and felt like a prisoner in her own bedroom—in her own home.

She was right about one thing for certain, he could easily overpower her.

Dominique was a high school sophomore and an elite athlete who lived to play football; he was the best runner in track and massive in size with a superior physique.

She didn't feel safe alone with him and knew that if he was determined enough, he could easily take what he wanted from her.

She got up off the floor, climbed back under her covers, and cried herself to sleep.

"Monica, I'm so sorry, baby," she heard a raspy voice whimper.

Monica's eyes sprung open to see her stepbrother in tears kneeling down beside her bed on the floor.

At first, she couldn't say anything, and only laid there stiff and fully exposed like a dissected biology frog.

She could tell by his wretched demeanor he was being truthful, but she couldn't bring herself to say that everything would be okay and she forgives him.

"But, I meant what I said, Monica. I am in love with you."

She believed him because maybe he really was in his own little twisted way, but being with him was out of the question no matter how it was asked.

Her dad and his mom were married, and just by the idea of them two being linked together through such an amalgamated holy union as marriage, it totally disqualified him from being anything other than her brother.

In her purview, being in opposition to her disposition was sordidly useless.

"Do you forgive me?" Dominique asked as he reached out for her hand.

Monica retracted instantly with a look of disgust.

Her reaction cut him deep within and the rejection

was unbearable as he struggled getting up from the floor.

Dominique softly kissed Monica's cheek and left her room, and moments later, she heard the front door slam.

She desperately wanted to get away and was growing anxious by the hour as time slowly ticked away.

She reached over and grabbed her cellphone to check the time.

It was a little after six in the evening and she was still exhausted.

She was confident that Dominique had left the house, but wondered for how long, and she really hoped and prayed her uncle would come to get her before he returned.

Pulling the covers over her head, Monica began crying until she finally fell asleep again.

The sound of a squeaky door opening followed by the shattering of glass, caused Monica's eyes to pop open.

Her room was pitch black, and she knew immediately that she had overslept, forgetting to call her uncle.

"Oh, no," she exclaimed in a whisper.

Monica quickly hopped out of bed, tiptoed over to her bedroom door, and softly closed it.

She eased on the lock and quietly tiptoed back to her bed and slipped under the covers.

She could hear Dominique rustling around the house, bumping into things, and mumbling to himself.

Upon hearing his footsteps pause at her door, she stood up in bed, backed up against her headboard and stood as still as a British Knight on guard duty.

Dominique was there, standing outside her door.

He tried twisting the knob, but quickly realized that the door was locked and Monica had locked him out.

He became enraged and began beating violently on the door.

Monica was petrified, and each thrust at the door sent her sinking deeper and deeper into a timorous retreat.

Suddenly, everything grew quiet and she began to descend back down onto her bed relieved.

The very next moment changed everything as her door flew open, and the enraged Dominique charged her, slamming her head back into the corner of the headboard—knocking her unconscious.

Monica trembled in the dark—curled up in a fetal position on the floor at the foot of her bed, devastated.

Dominique was sitting on the foot of the bed beside her.

He was filled to the rim with unrelenting remorse for what he had just done to his stepsister.

"I'm so sorry, Monica," he kept repeating over and over again as she laid there speechless, beyond benumbed in deep exasperation.

Monica had been defiled, and desecrated like a looted tomb.

She reeked of alcohol, as well.

The scent was all over her; his scent was all over her, and disgust had positioned itself fully inside her.

"Monica?" he called out then reached out for her.

"Don't," she snapped; "Get out of my room," she demanded.

Dominique stood up in a drunken stupor and headed for Monica's bedroom door.

He paused in the doorway, turned back to her, and mumbled before leaving, "I do love you, Monica and it was not my original intent to ever assault you this way."

Monica's face burned and heavily displayed her rage.

She gritted her teeth, rushed to the door yelling, and slammed it in his face.

"Ugh," she yelled and started breaking and slanging things around her room.

She yanked the covers off the bed and flipped her mattresses over, snatched up the bed sheets along with the sleep-tee and panties she was wearing, and stuffed it all in the bathroom wastebasket.

As her fit of rage subsided, she drew a bath, got inside the steaming water, and sat there troubled in tears for hours.

"Monica?" she heard her father call out at daybreak.

He had entered her bedroom and was shocked to see it in disarray.

He looked around the room in confusion, wondering what on earth had happened while they were gone.

He called out for his daughter again and notice water on the floor of her bathroom.

When Pastor Dupree walked inside the bathroom, he was stunned to see his daughter sitting in the bathtub stupefied and naked.

"Monica? What happened in here?" he asked

Monica didn't answer, or bothered turning in his direction to acknowledge his presence.

"It reeks in here. Your bedroom smells like a bar and there's vomit on your floor. Did y'all throw a shindig or something, and got plastered with friends while we were away?" he asked, but an answer didn't follow his question.

Pastor Dupree walked closer to the tub staring at his daughter intently and notice that she had checked out.

Sticking his finger inside the tub, he became alarmed because the water was freezing, but his little girl wasn't shivering.

"Monica, get out of the tub, honey," he asked as he grabbed a towel to wrap her in.

She turned to him as tears began to free fall from her face.

"Come on now, sweetheart. Let me help you out of there," he insisted with great concern.

Monica obeyed her father and allowed him to help.

She stood in the doorway of the bathroom and watched as Pastor Dupree put her mattresses back on the bed frame and straightened her bed up, then he motioned for her to take a seat.

"Come over here right now, Monica. I want an explanation for this destruction site you call your bedroom."

Monica walked over and did what her father asked.

"Did you do this to your room?"

"Yes."

Would you like to tell me why?"

"No."

"Okay, then. Tell me anyway."

Monica looked up at her father and frowned before asking, "Why won't you go ask your son, Satan, you address as, 'Dominique?' "

Pastor Peter Dupree stood staring at her completely confused.

"He took in a deep breath, "Monica, just tell—."

"He raped me," she simply mumbled, cutting him off.

"What?"

Monica stood up and repeated what she said, "You heard me correctly, daddy. The bastard boy you took in, accepting as your own son, knocked me unconscious and raped me."

Her father shook his head in unbelief.

"I don't believe that, Monica. It's not in Dominique's nature to do such a thing. If you're upset about us leaving for that cruise, just say that, but don't spread malicious lies about folks for attention—."

"Get out of my room, dad," she cut him off and mumbled with no expression.

He stared at his daughter for a brief moment, shook his head, and scoffed giving in to her demand.

Monica maintained her composure, got dressed, and searched the destruction site for her cellphone to call her uncle.

She spilled her guts over the phone telling him everything that had happened and then packed all of her belongings.

As she gathered her things, she was abruptly disrupted by Pamela as she entered her bedroom in a fury.

"I dare you accuse my son of rape," she snapped as she walked up to Monica.

"He told me everything about what happened while we were away for the weekend. You seduced him, didn't you?" Pamela asked shaken in rage.

"You prance around this house with these tight short skirts and fitted tops, flipping your hair, glossing your lips, and batting your eyelashes to entice him. He is a man, Monica, exactly what did you expect would happen? Don't go off lying on my baby boy because you're easy."

Monica didn't respond to Pamela, thinking to herself asking, "What's the use?"

"So what do you have to say for yourself, Monica?" Pamela asked standing in front of her with her hands on her hips waiting on an explanation.

Monica looked up at Pamela with a raised eyebrow and smirked before simply stating, "Nothing."

"What do you mean by, 'Nothing?' Is that all you have to say?"

"Yep, that's it."

Pamela stood speechless.

It takes two people to argue and Monica decided that arguing with Pamela simply wasn't worth her time and energy.

Besides, she'd been through enough over the past forty-eight hours and it's hard to pour into something that's already overflowing.

Suddenly, a knock on the door interrupted their quiet time.

"What are you doing here, Patrick Lee?" Monica heard her father ask her uncle as he opened the door to let him in.

"I came to get my niece and all of her belongings." Patrick responded.

Monica grabbed a few of her bags and walked around Pamela leaving her standing there still speechless.

"You can't just take my daughter from here," the pastor protested.

"And, why not? You know exactly why I'm here so if you don't want the cops involved, you are best to leave me alone. I'm taking your daughter 'just' like that, and it ain't a fool in his or her right mind who's gonna try to stop me," Patrick stated more so as a warning and headed to

Monica's bedroom to help grab her things.

Pastor Dupree stood beside his wife and stepson in silence while Patrick and Monica walked back and forth putting her things on the back of his Chevy.

After they were done, Patrick stood in the doorway with Monica, winked at her, and then gave her a compassionate smile.

He turned back around as if he'd forgotten something and looked at his brother and his wife in disgust before addressing their son who was trying desperately not to make eye contact.

"Dominique François, come here, boy," Patrick demanded as Dominique did exactly as he commanded.

Patrick squeezed on tightly to Dominique's shoulder almost to the point of crushing it and threatened him.

"If you ever lay your filthy fingers on my pumpkin again, I will murder you, your mother, along with my brother. And son, I own a significant amount of land, animals and weapons of mass destruction—to properly dispose of a body without leaving a trace of evidence. So, I assure you that no one will ever find y'all's remains."

Patrick looked back up at his brother and his wife again and smiled before asking, "What?" Followed by, "I mean what I say and I'm a man of my word. Isn't that right, Pastor Pete? I'm glad I only share your reflection and not your character, twin brother."

Patrick finally let Dominique's arm go and shoved him to the floor and smiled down at him in great satisfaction.

Patrick reach and grabbed the brim of his hat and gestured good riddance, politely turned around, grabbed Monica by the hand, and left the residence with his only niece.

As Monica abandoned her memories, she was surprised to see Desirée leaning up against the doorframe of the study.

She smiled at Monica before explaining why she was there.

"The Lord said, 'I will give you a new heart, and a new

spirit. I will take out your stony heart, and give you a tender, loving heart,' but I suspect you already know the scripture with your dad being a preacher and all," Desirée said as she stepped on in the room.

"God didn't reveal to me what's wrong with you, Mon', but I can literally feel the pain in your heart as if it were my own. The Lord said to me that you will tell me yourself when you're ready to talk about it," Desirée continued on explaining.

"Your heart has hardened, but God asked me to come pray for you and that is why I'm here. He said to me, 'Go, and I will heal her heart, Desirée,' " she revealed as she knelt down in front of Monica to pray.

"Tia is gonna help," she said as Letitia walked in the room.

"Yep, you know that ancient saying that goes, 'When two or more gather in my name, there I am in the midst of them,' or, something like that," Letitia joked.

Monica choked back tears.

She felt lucky to have found two amazing friends like Letitia and Desirée who she was now sure wasn't in her life by chance, but by divine guidance and reason.

As they prayed fervently for her, The Lord did exactly what He said He'd do and wholly healed her heart.

She could tangibly feel His goodness and grace as it wrapped around her like a garment spreading peace within her.

Finally, The Lord her God whispered in her ear and called her, "Daughter," and then gave rest to His beautiful beloved.

9...BEAUTY'S REST

"Then Jesus said, 'Come to Me,

all of you who are weary and carry heavy burdens,

and I will give you rest.' "

—*Matthew 11:28 (NLT)*

"Dark Sleeping Beauty? How long are you planning on sleeping for, huh? How much beauty rest does one person need, anyway?"

Monica opened her eyes to see a tall muscular broad shouldered guy with almond colored skin, a tapered fade and adventurous brown eyes that reminded her of fun, squatting down in front of her.

He unexpectedly provided a marvelous smile that warmed her brand new heart.

"Who are you?" She asked curiously while smiling back at him.

Her smile made his heart leap, totally disrupting his thoughts.

"I'm, umm—I'm Xavier," he answered after he settled down his thoughts.

"Tia's Brother?" Monica asked then waited on him to confirm.

Xavier turned away for a second and laughed before answering, "Yes, I am."

"Well, hi, Xavier. I'm Monica. Now, where are your bedside manners? Why won't you help a girl up?"

Xavier extended his hand to Monica unable to take his eyes off of her curves as his mouth hung open.

"Monica, has anyone ever told you that you are too fine?"

Monica laughed and found Xavier extremely charming.

"Do you hit on all of your sister's friends?"

"Girl, no. Just the too fine ones," he joked.

"You're smooth, I see."

"But, rough around the edges," he said adding to her comment.

"I think I'm gonna like you a lot, Tia's brother," she admitted with a flirtatious look.

"Good, I was so hoping you'd say that," he said blushing.

Looking up at the clock up on the wall Monica asked, "So where's your sister, anyway on this late afternoon?"

"Getting dressed. We're having a celebration with a bang tonight. Tia, our little brother, Houston Jr, and I are going shopping to buy all of the details for this party, so hopefully she don't spend all afternoon in her bathroom.

Xavier took a good look at Monica and smiled.

"Now, back to you, dark chocolate. When was the last

time you've gotten some fresh air?"

"Ha, good question," she responded as she left the room, ran down the wrought iron spiral staircase, and headed for the terrace.

Xavier gleamed with admiration as he headed down the stairs after her.

"It supposed to be freezing this time of year, but Texas weather is so bipolar, but every so often it acts normal and has a really good day, and today is one of those days, X-man. Not bad for the last day of the year, wouldn't you say so, yourself?" she turned to ask Xavier.

"X-men?" He asked smirking.

"No, 'X-man,' " she corrected and giggled.

Monica turned back to look over the wrought iron railing from Letitia's terrace before admitting, "Your sister's loft is lovely and Dallas is a beautiful city I must say. Not quite Copperas Cove, though."

Xavier admiringly watched Monica as she talked.

He was spellbound by her pleasant voice.

She was rather soft spoken and he didn't care at all what she talked about, as long as she kept talking to him.

He desperately wanted to get to know her better.

"Monica, would you like to ride with us to get the food, drinks, and décor for the party?"

Xavier asked interrupting her rant and rave.

"I'm still recovering from a breakdown, X-man. I don't have the strength to hang out yet. I need to rest," she truthfully admitted.

"I've only been vertical for about ten minutes and I'm already exhausted from just being out here."

Xavier looked at Monica a little concerned for her because she did seem to look a little fatigue.

"Hey, come here, Monica," he requested, "I'm going to help you back upstairs before you end up fainting.

"Monica gave him a coy smile as he took her arm and wrapped it around his neck and assisted her back up the staircase.

"You're so sweet and so fine yourself, X-man," she said

flirting.

He tried to hide his blushing cheeks as he carefully helped her lay back down to rest before heading back towards the door.

"Hey, X-man?" Monica said calling out after him.

Xavier quickly turned around to see what she wanted.

"Thanks for the breath of fresh air," she commended, and not really talking about being out on the terrace at all, but referring strictly to his kindness.

Xavier smiled and nodded then headed back down the stairs to wait in the car with his baby brother until Letitia finished getting dressed.

Monica was up and down throughout the day and on into the night as they brought in the New Year.

She couldn't explain why she was so drained, but still, somehow, felt so free.

Perhaps, it was because Monica had an uncountable amount of sleepless nights over the years, anxious about everything under the sun, but God had taken her weariness away, and her burdens leaving rest in its place.

As friends and family left Letitia's loft for the night, Monica grabbed a blanket and made her way through the sliding doors that led to the terrace.

She had discovered that she loved being out there.

She found it pleasant, peaceful, and perfect.

Monica wrapped herself inside her comforter and relaxed under a canopy on a chaise lounger enjoying the fresh cool air.

"So, here is where you snuck off too? I hadn't been completely honest with you about why I came into the study to meet you earlier today," Xavier confessed as he walked out on the terrace.

Monica sat up to listen to what he had to say.

"I talked to Tia earlier today about you. When she told me who you were, I expressed my interest in you, but she told me you and I can't see each other. She said that if you showed any interest in me it probably wouldn't be real. She also said I'm not your type which confuses me because I've been flirting with you all evening and night with no objections from you."

Monica put her head down a moment before answering, "I think you're sweet Xavier. Honestly, I really do, but."

"But? 'But' what? What does that even freakin' mean, Monica?" Xavier snapped in desperate need for his question to be answered quickly.

"I'm not sure, X-man," she lied.

"It's too complicated to explain," Monica answered without any solid clarification.

"Do you like me?"

"Yes, I do."

"Then, uncomplicate the reason for me please because I need an answer and I need it sooner than later."

"Is 'Uncomplicate,' even an actual word?" She asked in an attempt to change the subject.

"And, who on earth even cares?" Xavier asked frowning.

"I think it is a word, but only if you add a, 'D' at the end, making it 'Uncomplicated' instead." Monica added pretending to be deep in thought.

"Monica, just answer the question and stop beating on the bush," he snapped.

She looked up at him and laughed.

"It's, 'beating around the bush,' " she corrected.

Xavier looked over at Monica, irritated and snapped at her again, "No one even cares. The bush is still taking a beating."

Monica fell out laughing before buttering him up.

"Has anyone ever told you that you look so hot when you're irritated?" Monica asked as she got up from the chaise and stepped up on the railing beside him.

She took some of her comforter to share with him by handing him the corner to pull it around his shoulders.

Xavier blushed unable to hide the fact he liked her and her charming ways of getting off the topic and under his skin.

She crossed her arms and leaned over resting her head on his shoulder.

"Okay now, X-man. Ask me the question again. This time do it with more heated passion so I will be more likely to answer."

"Girl, you done made me forget my doggone question."

Monica giggled and wrapped her arm around his back.

It prompt him to pull her closer as she snuggled up under him, he closed his eyes, and exhaled with a blissful smile dominating his face.

"I really like you a lot, Monica."

"I really like you, too."

"My sister is clueless about you, dark beauty. She don't know you at all. Of course, you're in to me," he affirmed to assure himself mostly.

Monica giggled again, but didn't verbally respond to his comment.

She had no clue what she was doing with Xavier in the moment and it felt strange being under a guy, but somehow it also felt natural.

She knew in her perfect new heart that the feeling she was feeling for Xavier was the feeling God had intended for a woman to feel for a man all along.

It all seemed rather strange.

She had spent years being bitter about what Dominique had done to her.

It had put her in a bad place where she couldn't receive a man's affection for her even her uncle, Patrick.

There is no one that Monica loves more than Patrick, but whenever he'd reach out to embrace her she'd flinch.

Any kind of physical contact would set her off, especially wrestling and horse playing.

Patrick would often take Monica with him to baseball games.

One time, Monica, knowing how much her uncle loves baseball and his baseball caps, snatched one off his head at a game and took off running.

It was all fun and games as he chased her around the stands to take his favorite cap back, and they laughed so hard at the fact of him not being able to catch her.

However, when her uncle finally caught up with her, he playfully grabbed her from behind in a bear hug, knocked her down, and tried prying his cap from her hands, but Monica went ballistic in the middle of the baseball game.

Patrick knew the reason, but couldn't explain it to the crowd of people there who had witness the entire incident and heard her screams.

She remembered what China had told her once about the hold that Dominique had over her because of what he had done and she realized in that moment that China was right.

Dominique had stolen something that was priceless and she couldn't ever get it back and because of what one guy had done to her, the rest that remained didn't stand a chance with her.

Something took place the night before that completely changed that.

Although she completely remember what Dominique had done, she wasn't bitter about it at all, and better than that, she wasn't angry at Dominique anymore.

It's a victory that she would have to claim every day in order for it to be maintained which is always important.

When God heals you, especially from emotional wounds because they penetrate your heart, soul, mind, and spirit, but when those issues arise again, and they will, it's only the enemy trying to remind you of your past —a past that you are no longer bound to.

It's your responsibility to get up everyday and put on the full armor of God so that you would be able to stand firm against his strategies, and Monica will have to learn that one day at a time.

Monica closed her eyes and smiled as her head rested against his chest.

She could hear his heart pounding and knew it was

because of her.

"This feels nice and so right," Xavier whispered.

"Yeah, it really does," she agreed.

"If Tia finds out she is gonna be furious."

"Yep, that's for sure."

Xavier grinned hard exposing all of his teeth.

"So that means you're interested in me, huh?"

"Of course not, I only date cute guys," she joked.

"Ooh, that's cold," he responded laughing.

"How old are you anyway, X-man?" She curiously asked as she looked up at him.

"I'm seventeen."

"Wow, you're still in high school?"

"Yeah, but I ain't no student," he flirtatiously assured.

"Hmm, a very impressive, comeback."

Monica laughed and rested her head back on his chest.

"We can't tell my sister about us, you know."

"I know, I'm way ahead of you"

10...TAKEN ABACK

"Cling to your faith in Christ, and keep your conscience clear.
For some people have deliberately violated their consciences;
As a result, their faith has been shipwrecked."

−1 Timothy 1:19 (NLT)

"Where have you been?" Amberlee shouted with her hands on her hips as she entered her grandfather's former home with Kimberlee to pickup Monica and return to LCU.

"Hey, Amber. Why won't you just barge right on in without knocking or speaking first and bring your twin inside with you to do the same thing, please," Monica suggested with sarcasm.

"This is our grandfather's house. We don't need permission to come in," Kimberlee tried reminding after stepping out from around her sister.

"Yeah, you're partially right, but he is the same grandfather who willed his house to me before he died which makes me the sole beneficiary of this here estate which gives me the right to introduce you to the other side of the door and off my property."

Desirée, who was sitting comfortably on the sofa waiting on Monica to finish packing her things before heading back to campus, lowered her head and snickered.

Kimberlee looked at Desirée and snapped at her.

"Is something funny to you?"

"Of course, not." Desirée quickly responded and lost her smile.

Amberlee looked over at Desirée curiously before

asking politely, "And, who are you, if I may ask?"

"Oh, I'm Ré," Desirée answered with a different kind of smile.

"Like it even matters," Kimberlee snapped again.

"Why aren't you already packed to head back to the campus, Monica? Amber and I aren't waiting all morning for your black behind."

"You won't have to, lovely cousins because I'm not riding with y'all," Monica informed.

Amberlee looked at Kimberlee in wonderment.

"Monica, why not? Amberlee asked, "We always ride back together."

"Not this time," Monica assured her, "Because, I'm riding back with my friends, Ré and Tia."

"But, you and Letitia aren't friends anymore," Amberlee tried reminding her frowning.

"Correction, we are friends and like I said already, I'm riding back to the college with her and Desirée."

"Well, aren't you just a trending trader and very

unexpectedly, too, I might add," Kimberlee added verbalizing her opinion.

Monica looked confused.

"And, just what is that supposed to mean?"

"You didn't show up for our family Christmas party or the New Year traditional celebration at the manor."

Monica couldn't believe what she was hearing as an excuse for calling her a trader, and for Kimberlee to say she was trending as if it had been going on for weeks, was an exaggeration.

She understood how Kimberlee could be so self-centered, but it was shocking and totally beneath Amberlee.

Monica stopped packing and crossed her arms before responding.

"Have either one of you thought for a second to drop by my house and check up on me, pick up the phone to call, or do the simplest thing as ask y'all's dad how I've been doing?"

Monica waited for an answer and when one didn't come, she answered her own question.

"Of course you all didn't. Neither one of you have a clue and could probably care less about what I've been through this past week."

"What's that's supposed to mean," Amberlee asked.

"I knew it wouldn't be long before this black country house Barbie starts thinking she's better than us," Kimberlee expressed.

"Is that true, Mon'?" Amberlee asked, "You think you're better than us, now?"

"What? Do you two even hear yourselves? That has nothing to do with anything I'm saying."

"Well, what are you saying, Monica? Because, all I'm hearing is gibberish about my character," Amberlee asked and admitted.

"It's not like that," Monica tried explaining.

"Then, explain to me, at the least, how it is," Amberlee demanded.

"I'm just trying to find myself and my own way of doing things, that's all. I feel that it's time for me to start making friends instead of clinging to you two, and your friends, all the time. Not to mention the belittling Kim likes to inflict whenever she gets bored with herself. Riding with other girls my own age sounds like a safe, healthy, and better option," Monica explained with sincerity.

Monica stood up and grabbed the last of her bags.

"All ready and packed to go, Ré. Let's head on out," she announced before walking around her cousins leaving them standing in the living room with egged faces.

"Wait, Monica," Amberlee asked grabbing her by the arm.

"What did you go through this past week that we don't know about?" She asked with a sincere heart.

Monica smiled at her cousin with hope, but before she could say anything, Kimberlee cut her off.

"Amber, stop pacifying this tar baby and go ahead and

let her ride with Deshyra and Lateeka. We don't care."

Monica looked at Kimberlee as tears blurred her vision and swallowed hard without saying anything.

Desirée couldn't take anymore and had, had enough.

"Okay, that's enough," she said as she grabbed Monica by the wrist to pull her on out the door.

"Girl, shut up and move. You're not a part of this family so stay out of our family affairs," Kimberlee told her.

"You are so misguided," Desirée responded in amazement.

Monica still stood there staring.

She couldn't understand why Kimberlee hated her so much.

It had been going on for years, and she was growing tired of it.

Kimberlee had told her once before that she was unlovable and a man wouldn't ever marry her because she was too dark and no man wants extra black babies and have to look at them everyday.

For the longest time she believed her.

Monica went back to that day in her mind as she stared a Kimberlee in disbelief that her own flesh and blood could make her life so miserable and she hadn't ever done anything to deserve it.

"What's the big deal? It's just skin," she whispered softly to herself as she stared at her reflection in the mirror.

"It's not my skin that makes me—'me.' It's what's on the inside that matters," she tried convincing herself after Kimberlee tried convincing her that no man would ever want her.

Monica sighed and reached into her purse and fumbled around until she found what she was looking for.

She pulled out a black eyeliner and wrote a huge X across the bathroom mirror, and despised the color of her skin from that day forward.

She continued staring at Kimberlee as she dismissed

her memory.

"What have I done to you that has caused you to hate me for all of these years, Kim?" Monica asked searching Kimberlee's eyes for an answer hoping she'd find one there just in case her twisted twin cousin decided not to give her one.

Kimberlee's face wrinkled with disgust as she walked closer to Monica.

"Are you serious? I can care less about you, Jigaboo."

Desirée, tried her hardest to try to read Kimberlee, but what she felt coming from her was pure hatred, and not for Monica at all, but for herself.

"You hate yourself?" Desirée asked.

Kimberlee looked in Desirée's direction with great repugnance.

"Didn't I tell you to shut up?" Kimberlee asked with cold eyes.

Desirée walked closer as she realized she was right.

"You don't just hate yourself, but you secretly wished a

part of you didn't exist, and Monica reminds you of that part," Desirée revealed.

"I'm not going to tell you to shut up again because next time you say something to me, I'm going to shut you up with my fist," Kimberlee threatened.

Desirée turned to face Monica, took her by the hand, and smiled softly at her.

"Your cousin despises you because you remind her of the part of herself that she hates. The poor girl hates being black, that's all. I know it sounds silly because I'm sure there's a lot of other folks with a significant amount of melanin in their skin that's in your family, but you have the most so looking at your really dark complexion is a constant reminder that she's black too—no matter how light her skin is."

Kimberlee became enraged and had reached her boiling-point as she pushed Desirée in the back of the head knocking her down to the floor.

"Didn't I tell you to shut up?!" Kimberlee yelled.

Desirée got up from the floor and smiled at Kimberlee in delight before reassuring, "I rest my case. She hates herself because she's black."

Monica looked at Kimberlee astounded.

"Is that all you see when you look at me, Kim? You see what you hate about yourself? For years, I've paid the price for your mom and dad's love for each other that created you?"

"I could care less, or maybe I could which wouldn't matter anyway. To answer your stupid question would imply that I care, which I don't so get out my face before I hit you in yours," Kimberlee responded.

Amberlee was speechless.

She loves Monica, but Kimberlee comes first and always has.

No matter how much bad Kimberlee did or how selfish she had been, Amberlee stood by her side and took up for her at all cost and this day wouldn't be any different.

"That's pretty farfetched, don't you think, girl Ré?"

Amberlee asked suspiciously.

"I'm not wrong," Desirée assured her.

"But our father is dark, so it makes no sense. I mean not as dark as Monica, obviously, but nevertheless he's still somewhat dark."

"Your father, literally, 'pale' in comparison to Monica's complexion," Desirée pointed out.

"I'm done and I've had enough. Ré, please, let's just go," Monica urged as she turned back around to leave.

At the door, she paused and turned to face Kimberlee.

"It's really too bad that all you see when you look at me is my darkness because inside, I'm filled with marvelous light, and no matter how dark my skin is—it can't even begin to be compared to the darkness that resides on the inside of you."

Monica turned her back to her twin cousins after asking them politely, "Please lockup my house when you two leave."

As Monica sat down on the passenger side of Desirée's

Jeep Wrangler, she released the tears she had been holding inside.

"I am completely blown away, Ré."

"I know," Desirée responded in sympathy.

Although Desirée was able to put together Kimberlee's feelings, she still had a few missing pieces that were still left out.

She wondered why Kimberlee hated being black.

"You know something, Monica. My mom was white and my dad was black, too. I love both parts of me—equally. Racism is such stupidity," she expressed.

"Amber and Kim's mother, Faye abandoned them when they were very young," Monica began explaining.

"Faye abandoned her family when they didn't approve of her marrying my uncle, Patrick. After several years of being married, she discovered she didn't love him anymore. All they did was fight anyway," Monica admitted.

"Faye made up her mind to leave for good, but she'd be

leaving with just the clothes on her back because of a prenup she signed. Faye's mother told her she could come back, but she couldn't bring her black daughters with her. So, she left them and moved back home with her parents."

"Well, that explains it then and that is why she hates being black because they were rejected by their mother's side of the family," Desirée said as she put together the rest of the pieces with Monica's assistance.

"You'll get better at standing up to them the more you stand up for yourself," Desirée assured her, "Sometimes you have to dig deep to try and understand people in order for you to forgive them, too."

"I guess you're right but I'm still taken aback with this whole matter," Monica admitted.

"Well, my suggestion is, don't allow your cousins to cause you anymore angst," Desirée told Monica before she encouraged her.

"Look at it this way—know that there's going to be

trouble produced by high winds. Often times, the waters may even be troubled, and although you are taken aback by the strong currents, brace yourself like a ship a sail does, and trust that the masts and spars, the Lord has put around you, will support you. We have your back, Monica, always and that's a promise."

11...TIES THAT BLIND

"What is causing the quarrels and fights among you?
Don't they come from the evil desires at war within you?"

—*James 4:1 (NLT)*

Monica opened her eyes, in response to a banging at the door followed by cursing.

She quickly got out of bed to relieve the annoying hand that wouldn't give her dormitory door a break.

Swinging the door open, there stood Kimberlee Dupree wearing temperament and resentment.

Monica rolled her eyes, and walked away from the door leaving her standing there to let herself in.

"Now isn't the time for dramatics, Kim," Monica remarked as she laid back down on her side and pulled her covers up to her neck.

"Well, you better make time because I'm more than outraged at that little stunt you pulled yesterday. Now, look at me in my face and explain to me why you chose Letitia's side over me and Amber's.

Kimberlee stood in front of her smoldering waiting on her to answer.

"I don't have to answer to you. Go back to your dorm room before I call our dorm mom and let her know you're harassing and trying to bully a freshman."

Kimberlee was no longer smoldering as her anger ignited into a full blown flame.

She snatched Monica covers from around her causing her little cousin to roll out of bed onto the floor.

"You will answer me so get up off the floor, right now

and tell me to my face why you chose Letitia's side over your own family," Kimberlee demanded.

Monica scoffed as she slowly stood to her feet.

"Didn't I tell you yesterday that we're no longer family?" Monica ask Kimberlee.

"Actually, I've already dragged you over to the waste basket icon and with a simple right click, I've permanently deleted you from my memory."

"Monica, I am so close to dragging you around this room by your hair until I yank out every single strand from your scalp," she threatened.

"Ha! Do you and sanity even know each other?" Monica asked with false astonishment.

"You prove everyday that there's no method to your madness and that you're just mad, all the time, for no apparent reason at all. So, okay. Since you wonna know so badly, then I'll tell you," Monica told her as she scoffed again.

"I helped Tia because you and Amber have some

nerve cornering her in an attempt to jump her. That was a coward's move and I'm so glad I didn't ride back to the campus with y'all or else she would've thought that I had something to do with it.

Kimberlee was upset at Monica because of the failed attempt to get even with Letitia for making a fool out of her on countless occasions.

Kimberlee was supposed to have graduated already with Amberlee before Monica had even decided to start college after wanting to wait a year after high school, but because of Kimberlee's poor academic performance, repeating the courses she failed, was her only option.

Although Amberlee had already graduated, she still found it hard to move on as Kimberlee always had some sort of drama going on at the campus that she always found herself in the middle of, such as this time.

Amberlee had driven Kimberlee back to Lubbock and she talked her into luring Letitia into a trap, jump on her, and leave her beaten, bruised, alone, and frightened.

The plan failed when Monica sensed something wasn't right when she saw Amberlee's canary yellow BMW still parked in the visitor's parking lot, and she wondered why she hadn't left yet.

She knew about the drama that had unfolded before the holiday break and that Kimberlee wasn't going to just drop it.

Monica search the campus for her cousins with the full knowledge of knowing they were up to something.

Walking around to the isolated back side of the dormitory units, she could hear her cousins arguing with Letitia.

Monica became furious when Amberlee had pushed Letitia and she saw that Kimberlee was going forward to do the same.

Monica found courage that she never knew she had as she ran to Letitia's defense and charged Kimberlee.

Hence the reason for Kimberlee being in her dorm room in full offense demanding she pray tell.

Monica exhaled in her exhaustion before addressing Kimberlee again.

"Aren't you tired of being a bully, Kim? You are unhinged, unhealthy, and unhappy wanting everyone else to be inhuman—just like you. When will you come to the realization that you are pitiful and broken?"

"You look haughty and down on me like you're any better, Monica?"

"I never claimed to be better—just different, and no longer diffident because of you. I've surpassed your pettiness, Kim. Can't you see that? I no longer need validation from you or anyone else for that matter. I'm at liberty to say that now, Monica explained with a whole new outlook.

"I remember my freshman year in high school and how I used to do anything you told me to in hopes you'd accept me and like me because of my devotion to my family," she continued explaining to Kimberlee.

"I found myself beginning to do the same thing now

my freshman year in college, but no more, Kim. I'm no longer a pawn in your game of chess, occupying space until you find need to move me," Monica assured, no longer afraid to stand up for herself.

Kimberlee went back to Monica's freshman year in high school as she remembered all the evil acts against others she had talked her into doing.

"Tess thinks she's so slick," Kimberlee claimed as she slung her books inside her locker.

"What's the problem, sis?" Amberlee asked as she put in her combination to grab the textbook for her next class.

Monica was sitting on the floor in the hallway waiting for Amberlee to finish getting her things trying her best to ignore whatever drama Kimberlee had stirring up.

"She's gonna regret crossing me after I get finish with her," Kimberlee assured.

"And, Monica and I are still waiting for you to tell us just what you're babbling on about," Amberlee told her.

"She was supposed to hook me up with Nathan, but I just saw them in Mr. Ginseng's class all booed up," Kimberlee explained as she slammed her locker.

"So, why is that a big deal? It's not like you two are dating," Amberlee asked attempting to stay reasonable.

"We would've been by now if she wouldn't have sank her fangs into his neck," Kimberlee claimed.

"I hate that pretty little backstabber and she's gonna regret trying to get over on me because I'm gonna snatch all that pretty little hair out of her pretty little head," Kimberlee threatened.

Monica laughed at her cousin's "not so unusual jealousy" because she knew that by saying, I'm gonna snatch," she really meant, "I'm gonna get Monica to snatch."

"What is it that you want me to do, Kim?" Monica asked not wasting hardly anytime waiting.

"You have gym with her next period, Monica. I want you to snip that pretty little ponytail off and let's just see how she looks then when she can't slang that stupid thing from side to side for awhile," Kimberlee explained with an ominous look.

Monica, wanting so badly to be in Kimberlee's favor, agreed to go along with her evil scheme.

In gym class, Monica sat behind Tessa on the bleachers as Kimberlee instructed with the knowledge it would be an educational video being played for the Phys Ed., class assignment.

As soon as the instructor pressed play and dimmed the lights, Monica reached inside her backpack, pulled out a pair of scissors Kimberlee had given her, and slowly cut pieces of Tessa's hair little by little to avoid getting caught.

She then eased her way out of the gym to give the waiting Kimberlee the thumbs up that the mission was a complete success.

Everyone could hear Tessa's screams throughout the entire school when she discovered that someone had cut off all her hair, but the plan backfired.

When Tessa returned to school the next day, everyone discovered she was just as pretty without her extremely long hair and as it turned out, Nathan liked her just as much with short hair.

"All those horrible things I did for you and I was blind to think you'd accept me as family, but I was being a fool," Monica admitted tearfully as Kimberlee thoughts returned to the present.

"You're just looking for someone else to blame for the evil deeds that you have always been capable of doing— but, you're not using me as your scapegoat," Kimberlee remarked.

"I don't need a scapegoat, billygoat, or any other kind of goat for that matter," Monica wittily assured her.

"The majority of your evil plans fail, leaving you looking like the fool all on your own."

"This whole family is full of fools," Monica thought to herself as she realized arguing with Kimberlee regarding anything was senseless and a bit repetitive.

Kimberlee was over Monica and was about to go all in for a cutthroat comeback.

"I know an evil plan that didn't fail," she said grinning.

"And, what's that?" Monica made the mistake of asking.

The one when your mother died.

Monica could taste the salt from her tears as they came pouring down her face.

She reached back and slapped Kimberlee so hard that it left a huge red swollen palm print across her face.

Kimberlee was dumbstruck as she stood staring in a stupor.

Monica gleamed with satisfaction through her tears as Kimberlee made one last attempt to threaten her.

"You've crossed me for the very last time. There won't be a next time because I plan to teach you a lesson once and for all."

Monica laughed aloud and asked, "Do you even hear

yourself? You're such a villain."

"You've crossed me for the last time. There won't be a next time because I plan to teach you a lesson once and for all," Monica retorted in a mockery.

"You have absolutely no class. What could you possibly teach me?" Monica asked teasing.

"You'll learn soon enough," Kimberlee promised as she left Monica's dorm slamming the door behind her.

12...BEATING HEARTS

"My lover tried to unlatch the door, and my heart thrilled within me."

—Song Of Solomon 5:4 (NLT)

"Hey, Dark Sleeping Beauty. Get up and pack your bags," Xavier told Monica over the phone from outside the female dormitories.

"Meet me outside in the far parking lot away from your college campus. I'm here to drive you home for the weekend. We are about to have beaucoup fun in your hometown for a change in scenery."

"What am I going to tell, Tia and Ré this time?"

"You won't have to tell them anything because we're going to Copperas Cove so we won't have to dodge them all weekend like we do here in Lubbock."

Monica paused to take a deep breath trying to contain her excitement and still voice her unease.

"We've been together almost every weekend, for a few months now, X-man. We're gonna have to tell her we're dating soon because if she finds out about us on her own, it won't be pretty."

"Adrian knows about us and he has agreed to cover us on that end by keeping her weekends as busy as possible until we work up the nerves to tell her."

"What about, Ré?"

"I saw her leave with her sister, Jasmine and friend, Nicole."

"What about the drive, X? You're driving five hours back and forth. From Dallas to Lubbock is five hours and from Lubbock to Copperas Cove is going to be another five. That's putting a ton of miles on that classic lady you're driving."

"For you, baby, I'd drive ten hours or even twenty, back and forth every single day if it meant I could see you."

"That's smooth," Monica complimented and blushed.

"Don't worry about the classic lady, I rebuilt this 1970 Dodge Challenger, from the ground up, this car is in outstanding condition and perfectly top performance."

"Well, I'm glad you decided to skip the bragging," Monica said sarcastically while laughing.

"You're so insane, X-man, and I like you a lot. Why don't you put that CD case down and look to your left," Monica suggested as she smiled and waved.

"You're so beautiful, girl—dang," he told her cheesing.

"Where are your bags?"

"We're going to my house, X-man. Why would I need bags to go home?"

"Makes sense. Get over here and come give your man a hug," Xavier ordered as he got out of the car.

Monica giggled and ran into his arms.

"The next couple of days should be interesting," Monica predicted as she got inside and buckled the seatbelt around her waist.

"For sure," Xavier agreed.

"Girl, your people got some paper," Xavier exclaimed as they pulled up to Monica's country style white house.

"Who lives here with you?" He asked curiously.

"I live alone," she answered as she grabbed him by his shirt and pulled him inside.

"Now, get in here so I can kiss on you."

"You won't have to ask me twice," he assured and obeyed.

Xavier was impressed as he looked around the house, picking things up, and studying others.

The interest he had in Monica had stalker like qualities, but it was only because he wanted to know everything about her.

She peaked his interest to no end and Monica knew

that she'd have to let him in on private details about her life really soon.

Monica watched Xavier as he wandered up the stairs, snickering at her family photos, and cracking up at her baby pictures.

As he ventured off into her bedroom, she quickly went after him a little worried by what he might find, but he was intrigued by all things, "Monica" and he was anxious to know every solitary thing about her.

"Do you even own a pair of jeans?" Xavier asked amazed digging through Monica's closet.

"No, I do not," she responded as she snatched a satin slip from his hand.

"Explains why I've never seen you in a pair before," he remarked grinning.

"I bet you would look totally hot in a pair of denim jeans," he said thinking out loud.

"I've never even worn a pair of jeans—ever, and I probably never will."

Extremely curious, he asked her, "What's the story behind that anyway? I couldn't help but notice not one female in your family pictures have on jeans."

"Dupree women don't wear pants in my family. It's like this unwritten rule or something," she explained.

"Is it a religion or occult thing?"

"No, not at all. Maybe, you can say it's more of a cultural thing that's been part of my family for quite some time."

"Have you ever wanted to wear a pair?" Xavier curiously asked.

Monica thought long and hard for a moment and realized the thought never even crossed her mind.

"Not particularly—no," she truthfully admitted.

Xavier smiled and stared at his girlfriend as he tried picturing her in denim jeans.

"What?" She asked coyly.

"Let's go shopping, Monica," Xavier insisted with delight as he grabbed her by the arm and headed out the door.

Monica had to admit that she was ecstatic.

She's never owned a pair of jeans before or ever wanted to, but was curious to see how she'd look.

"X-man, I don't know what size I wear in pants," she admitted with a worried expression.

Xavier quickly looked over at his beautiful girlfriend sitting on the passenger side of his ride and as his eyes slowly followed down her long dark legs, he grinned.

Shifting to fourth gear, he shifted his eyes back to the road then licked his lips, and smirked before answering, "You're a ten."

Monica turned her head blushing as she stared out the window.

Xavier made her heart pound out of control.

It was a feeling she'd never experienced before and it felt nice; it felt right in that moment as she realized she was falling for him.

Nothing could have been more perfect for Xavier.

He was in his classic lady with his classy lady and it was all good.

Monica was nervous as she tried on different brands and styles of jeans.

She'd never been shopping with a guy before and trying to remain modest was growing increasingly hard as Xavier stood outside every dressing room anxiously waiting.

"Like I said—totally hot in a size ten," he said and approved.

Monica face glowed in blissfulness.

"How many pairs should I buy?"

"How many would you like?"

"I don't know."

Xavier was already a few steps ahead of her.

He'd taken care of everything as she changed in the dressing rooms picking every pair he liked that complimented her curves.

He stood up grinning before admitting, "I've already

purchased my favorite ones."

Walking up to his beautiful girlfriend, he wrapped his arms around her waist, slipped his hands in the back pocket of her brand new denim jeans, pressed closely up against her, and planted a kiss on her soft lips.

"Now, keep these on and let's go get some food," he insisted with satisfaction.

"X-man, I have to admit this day has been amazing, I can't remember ever having this much fun in one day."

"That's how I roll, Monica."

She leaned over with a flirtatious smile.

"Let's get our dinner to go and we can eat back at my house by the fireplace," she suggested.

"Girl, sounds great. Let's ride," he agreed grabbing her by the hand.

"So, let me get this straight. You have a screened in back porch with a built-in fireplace?" Xavier asked astonished.

"I inherited this house from my grandfather," she

explained.

"And, he just gave you a whole house?"

"Sort of, along with some other stuff too that I can't get until I turn twenty-one," she casually revealed like it wasn't a big deal.

"That's so awesome," Xavier exclaimed, "All I own is my Challenger and these huge awesome biceps."

Monica threw her head back laughing aloud with admiring eyes as Xavier posed and flexed.

"You're borderline vain," she joked as she reached out for him.

"Truthfully, X-man, this old country house may be impressive, but it's lonely being here alone," she revealed.

"It was willed to me out of sympathy, I believe. My grandfather felt like something of significance was owed to me for something else that was taken from me. In my uncle's eyes, I deserve this and so much more."

"Seriously? How so?" Xavier asked wanting details.

Monica put her head down and decided to change the

subject.

She knew she'd have to tell Xavier sooner than later, but didn't want to ruin their first whole weekend together with any sad stories.

"So, X—umm, let me show you how this fireplace works. I used to love being out here when I was younger. One or two burning logs can last all night," she said as she walked off with him trailing closely behind.

Xavier decided to let the topic go for now as he could tell the shift in her mood and he wasn't interested in creating any awkward silent moments between them so he followed her lead, instead.

Once they got the fire going, Monica changed into her nightgown and they snuggled up close on a wicker patio sofa to enjoy each other's company.

Monica could tell that Xavier was falling for her so she knew she'd have to tell him the truth.

From fear she may lose him, she hesitated.

He rubbed her back as she laid up against his chest

listening to his heart beat with her arms around his waistline.

"It's okay, Monica," Xavier said softly before she could utter a word.

"I'm not a fool. I know there's something you're having a hard time telling me and that's okay. When you're ready to talk about it, I'll be ready to listen and I can tell you two things for certain, though. First things first, It won't ever change the way I feel about you," he said and grew quiet.

Monica waited a few seconds on Xavier to finish his sentence, but after a few more seconds went by, she urged him to complete his statement.

"What's the second thing?" She curiously asked.

He smirked at her curious expression as she lifted her head to look at him.

"C'mon, X-man. What's the second?"

"I love you," he softly whispered.

With an illumined face, her heart flooded.

She knew she'd have to tell him her history before it went any further even if it meant him changing his mind about being with her.

"I've never dated a guy before, X," she quickly blurted out before she lost her nerves to do so.

He looked confused.

"Is that your secret? So, you haven't been with a guy."

"No, X. That's not what I'm saying," she told him as she stood up to face him.

"I've never had a relationship with a guy before."

"I'm still not seeing your point," he admitted.

Monica exhaled deeply before attempting to break it down even further.

"I've only had one serious relationship in my whole life and it was with another girl."

Xavier smiled.

He wasn't heavily affected by her confession at all.

Had it been anyone else, he probably would've asked to meet the ex-girlfriend, but this was Monica and he truly cares for her and isn't a least bit interested in sharing her with another.

"Come here, dark beauty." he politely demanded while reaching out for her.

Monica smiled back at him, came closer, and wrapped her arms around his neck.

Xavier softly kissed his girlfriend and whispered, "It doesn't change anything. I still want to be with you because—I love you."

Monica softly whispered back, "I love you, too."

As their lips locked, so did their souls.

Xavier is honestly and deeply in love with Monica, and her feelings for him are mutual.

He had rightfully earned a place inside her heart, and Monica wanted him there; she chose not to ignore the desire that had arose within her as she climbed up onto the wicker sofa, wrapped her long dark legs around his waist, and allowed him in.

13...UGLIEST BEAUTY

"But in that coming day no weapon turned against you will succeed. You will silence every voice raised up to accuse you. These benefits are enjoyed by the servants of the Lord; Their vindication will come from Me.

I, the Lord have spoken!"

—Isaiah 54:17 (NLT)

"This cannot, under any circumstances, be happening right now," Monica expressed in distress.

She couldn't pull her eyes away from a plastic stick she held in her hand that had a display window revealing two solid bold blue vertical lines.

"Lord, I repented for my fornication, why is this even happening to me?" She asked praying aloud.

"My dad is going to kill me, raise me from the dead, and kill me again," she whispered to herself.

It had been eight weeks, since her and Xavier's weekend rendezvous retreat.

Her cycle hadn't come and she couldn't hold any food down.

It didn't take a genius to figure out what was probably wrong with her.

Monica and Xavier still hadn't come open about their relationship and he would be arriving soon to see her on this afternoon.

Not only would she have to tell him, but she would have to tell everyone how she have been secretly seeing a high school senior, who hadn't quite turned eighteen yet, and who would soon be her baby's daddy.

She was startled by a banging on the door that caused

her to waste a cup of urine on the floor.

Looking around she came to the realization that she was in complete denial as she had taken a little over a dozen pregnancy tests and had apparently went insane hoping just one of them would be negative.

The banging continued as she struggled in a hurry trying to gather up all the evidence of her one night encounter with a boy.

"Just a moment," she yelled as she shoved all the contents spread out across the floor into a big brown paper bag.

"Monica, come now. You've been locked in your dorm all morning. We have a picnic this afternoon with Adrian and Ré," she heard Letitia yell from the other side of the door.

"Just a second," she managed to respond with a cracking voice.

Monica balled the brown bag up, shoved it into an old shopping bag from the mall, tied it tightly closed, and hid it underneath a pile of dirty clothes on the floor of her closet.

She tried straightening her face up before letting Letitia in.

"Why have you been acting so strange lately? Huh, Monica?" Letitia asked as she shoved her aside to enter her dorm room.

"You have been wearing pants too, Monica, staying gone all weekend long, being extremely secretive with whatever you've been doing and whoever you've been doing it with," Letitia accused.

"If it's a girl you're seeing, you don't have to hide her from me. I know your secret. Remember?"

Monica swallowed hard and didn't respond.

She was trying hard to hide the devastation on her face.

Not to mention it was heavily coated in guilt.

She and Xavier had been seeing each other for months now.

She wouldn't be able to hide it, anymore once her belly starts showing, and this day, when Letitia's little brother arrives she would have to break the news to him and they would have to break the news, together, to everyone else.

It was too much for her to bear.

"You're not sneaking off this weekend either, Monica. This picnic will happen. Adrian is trying to hook Ré up with his friend, Chase. That white boy is fine, girl—also, you are going to have to come out soon and tell everyone about your secret soon because—."

"What secret?" Monica interrupted and asked.

"About your liking chicks, Monica. Are you okay?" Letitia answered and then asked.

"Oh, yeah. Of course," she answered, "I'm fine."

"I'm just saying, girl, before he tries to find some guy to hook you up with," Letitia said laughing.

She had begun to tune Letitia's voice out of her head as her mind traveled back in time to eight weeks ago at her house in Copperas Cove.

Morning sun rays pierced through the curtains exposing the silhouette of Xavier's perfect masculine physique.

As Monica sat behind him in bed, she paid close attention to how his mood had changed from only hours before.

Around two o'clock in the morning, they took what they'd started outside on the patio—inside, and up the stairs to her bedroom.

She looked over at the clock on the nightstand, raised her knees up to her chest, and tucked her hair behind her ears.

"This silence is way too loud, X-man. I'm just saying," she said frustrated.

He was acting weird and it was starting to really irritate her.

"We went too far, Monica," he turned to her and said.

"Are you serious?" She asked frowning.

"And what did you think would happen if we spent the

whole weekend together?" She curiously asked.

"I didn't think it through," he honestly admitted.

"I made a vow of celibacy. I mean, this happened once before since then and I blamed it on alcohol—which was still wrong, but I have no excuse for my actions this time."

"Well, it was intoxicating," Monica joked.

"That's not funny, Monica. I'm so serious," he exclaimed as he stood to his feet to face her.

Monica's heart raced as anger burned to a crisp within her.

"You're really starting to piss me off, Xavier Shriver, which is not the smartest thing to do considering the literal hell I've been through," she snapped as she got up out of bed and stood only inches from his face.

"The first guy I ever fell for was murdered only a few feet away from me. I was knocked unconscious and raped by my brother. I fell in love with a girl and was with her for two years before she broke up with me and killed herself, and only months later, I attempted to do the same," Monica expressed with overwhelming grief, in tears.

"And now, the guy I am madly in love with is standing before me, telling me how the passionate love I expressed to him, was a terrible mistake that he wish he could take back. You have some nerve, Xavier!"

He stood before her—thunderstruck as bereavement flooded his heart.

The guilt he felt before, had died within him and sorrow for his girlfriend became the only emotion he could feel.

He knew God would forgive him for breaking his vow, but would Monica forgive him for breaking her heart?

"I didn't know all of that," he said in deep sadness.

Monica lowered her head and sighed as huge drops of tears dropped from her eyes and splatted like melted hot wax on the cherry oak hardwood floor beneath her feet.

"No, you didn't," she said softly as her fierce anger dissipated.

"It's not even your fault," she admitted as she took a seat on the edge of her bed.

"How could you have known?" Monica asked with her head down.

Xavier got on his knees in front of her on the floor.

He wrapped his arms around the disappointed beautiful dark Monica and whispered in her ear, "We'll get through this together."

She let go of all the disappointment, and allowed him to console her.

"It's Sunday morning. If you want to repent, my dad's service starts in about half an hour. Our church is only ten minutes away," she told him after he finally let her out of his loving embrace.

Xavier grinned before answering her.

"Girl, that sounds great. Not that I need to go to church to repent or anything, but it would be so nice to meet some of your family," he admitted.

"By the way, I know your dad is a southern Baptist

preacher and all, but I ain't tapping my neighbor on the shoulder to tell them nothing. So, he bet' not ask," he joked.

"You're so silly, X-man."

"Monica, are you gonna finish getting dressed for our afternoon lunch picnic with Adrian, or what?" Letitia asked ushering Monica back into the present.

"Oh—um, yeah. I'm wearing what I have on."

Letitia stepped back to take a closer look at Monica's attire.

"Are you sure?" She asked in disgust.

"You look like you just rolled out of bed, girl. Your shirt is wrinkled up and all bunched together like chitlins; you also have bed hair. Good thing those jeans look really nice and treating you right," Letitia told her snickering with her arms folded.

Monica rolled her eyes before going to her closet.

She slipped on another t-shirt, slid on some thong flip-flops, put on a Texas Rangers baseball cap, shoved her cell in the back pocket of her jeans, and proceeded out the dorm room.

"Whatever, snapback Gingersnap," Letitia mumbled and giggled as she closed Monica's dorm room door and followed her out of the building.

Monica couldn't think straight.

Those pregnancy tests were dominating her thoughts.

She kept thinking over and over in her mind, "Fifteen tests I took this morning, and not one of them had a negative result to, at the least, give me a single shred of hope."

Not to mention, Letitia and Desirée was acting silly getting on her last nerve.

She was treating them like it was their fault—she'd gotten herself into this mess that she didn't know how to find her way out of.

Her phone pinged and it startled her.

She quickly reached in her back pocket to check the message and was ecstatic to see it was Xavier texting to let her know he had made it to the college.

She was so distracted by the tests that she'd forgotten to text Xavier and warn him that they were all outside sitting under a tree on campus having an afternoon lunch, and if he parked out front in visitor's parking, the gang would surely see him.

Monica jumped up, excused herself, and quickly headed for his car before they'd recognized who he was, but it was too late.

They saw him and disapproval weighed Letitia's face down.

Monica and Xavier were busted.

"Bae, I was parked down there at first, over there under that oak tree and some stupid birds pooped all over the hood of my ride," Xavier said as he got out of his car to kiss his girl.

He snatched her by the bottom of her t-shirt, pulled her up against him, and kissed her before joking, "I think they're just hating on me because I'm flyer than them."

"Get it, Bae? 'Fly?' " Xavier asked laughing.

Monica looked worried as she threw her arms around him.

"Not now, X-man, she whispered, "Here comes your sister and she knows about us."

"Uh—oh," He whispered back as his expression changed while looking over Monica's shoulders at his blistering sibling.

Xavier, leaned up against his car and folded his arms as Letitia approached them.

"Y'all are some haters," he accused and scoffed.

"So, you all are dating? How long has this been going on, brother?"

"I thought I mentioned it to you, Tia," Xavier lied.

"You most certainly did not, Xavier Eugène Shriver,"

"Oh, I'm sorry, sis. I guess it was just Adrian I mentioned it to instead."

"Oh, really?" Letitia angrily asked as she turned to Adrian.

"Are we cool, Tia?" Monica asked pleading with her eyes for a yes.

"He's seventeen, and you're going to jail!"

"Is that true?" Monica asked wearing worry, "Can I really go to jail?"

Desirée, who had chosen Pre-Law as a major quickly answered, "That's not true."

"Shut-it-up, Pre-law," Letitia demanded.

"Tia, sis, please don't mess this up for me," Xavier pleaded.

"I love, Monica. I was wrong for hiding our relationship from you, but to be fair, we were going to tell you together, today, actually. I promise."

Letitia didn't respond to her brother, but instead, walked over to Monica and yanked her aside.

"Does my little brother know that you're not into guys?" Monica's eyes filled with tears as she whimpered, "That's not fair, Tia."

"Isn't it?" Letitia asked.

"He's a kid, Monica. He's still in high school, and besides, he deserves to know the truth about you."

"What's the truth about me? Because, I would really like to know myself. I'm not sure which I'm into, Tia, but I am sure about one thing and that's—I'm in love with your brother, Xavier," she confessed.

"You have to believe that and I know how old he is. But, so what? He'll be eighteen soon enough," she truthfully stated.

"Please say, we're cool, Tia."

"Do you really love him, Monica?"

"Yes, I really do."

Letitia put her head down, smacked her lips, sighed, and agreed, "We're cool."

"Thank you, Tia," Monica exclaimed as she threw her arms around Letitia's neck.

Monica looked over at Xavier and blew him a kiss.

One huge sigh of relief had been lifted off her shoulders, but there was another heavy weight that was still burdening her and she knew this one wasn't going to be so easily accepted.

Xavier walked over to his, "now known" girlfriend and kissed her, openly, for all to see.

"So, now what?" he asked her.

"Do you still wonna leave or chill here with my sister and friends for a first?"

"Let's finish this picnic before you check-in to your hotel. There's something important we need to discuss and we can do so after we leave the theater and have dinner."

Looking worried, he wanted to ask about the importance of the discussion, but judging from his girlfriend's unsettled expression, he thought it best to wait until later, just like she had suggested.

"I hate being away from you," Xavier expressed to Monica over dinner, in a not-so secluded restaurant.

It felt good to not hide their relationship anymore and she wanted to celebrate that by going to a more open and popular restaurant for a change, and there'd be no more hiding in dark far-off places right outside of town.

"I hate being away from you, too. I'm sorry long distance relationships suck so much," Monica responded.

"But, they don't have to suck, though. And, as far as hating them goes, you sure haven't been acting like it," Xavier angrily blurted out.

Monica placed her napkin in her lap while looking around, then leaned over to whisper, "Keep your voice down, X-man. What's going on with you, huh? You been acting weird ever since I mentioned to you that we need to talk."

He lowered his voice, but didn't release any tension from his face as he said to her, "You think that I don't know what, 'We need to talk' means? You're trying to breakup with me.

Monica grinned at her overly bothered boyfriend.

"You're such a 'guy,' X. So, is that the reason why you've been a sourpuss all evening?"

Still grinning, she reached her hand across the table, grabbed his hands, and spoke softly saying, "There's no way I'd ever consider breaking it off with you, especially after the discussion we're about to have."

Motioning for the waitress, she politely suggested to Xavier, "Let's get out of here."

While leaving the restaurant, if only they'd paid more attention to their surroundings, like they used to do, they could've possibly had a great chance of preventing a terrible thing, that was about to occur, from ever happening.

Someone was watching them and had been ever since they'd arrived at the restaurant.

"Now, what's so important that you insisted on waiting all fricking day to tell me?" Xavier asked as he opened the door for Monica to get in the car.

Monica didn't say anything right away, as she watched him walk around to the other side of his car to get in.

She remain quiet, still, as he started the car, buckled his

seatbelt, and drove off.

He was starting to worry again because she hadn't said anything yet and her silence was building up anxiety within him.

"Monica, please tell me that you aren't still upset about the celibacy thing."

She looked over at him and answered truthfully, "I wish to God it was that sim—."

"The vehicle behind us is extremely close." Xavier pointed out cutting her sentence off while looking in his rearview mirror.

"What?" Monica asked as she turned around to see what he was talking about just as the dark color SUV sped up to swerve into their car.

"Watch out!" Monica yelled before everything went dark.

14...TIME & SPACE

"You intended to harm me, but God intended it all for good.

He brought me to this position so I could save the lives of many people."

—Genesis 50:20 (NLT)

"Where am I?" Monica asked as she observed her surroundings standing in pure Light.

Although it was remarkably bright, it wasn't blinding.

She felt enraptured as The Light embraced her.

Monica softly simpered with her eyes closed.

The Light was alive and breathing; she could feel it all

around her and everywhere inside.

"Dark Daughter—full of Light, try to remember where you were," a still small voice whispered from within.

"I don't know, but I do remember being really happy," Monica recalled.

"You are, indeed, happy," the still small voice declared.

Immediately following the declaration, a field of fuchsia lilies appeared all around her.

Monica gasped at the beautiful scenery as it became increasingly overwhelming.

"This is happiness," she exclaimed.

"Fuchsia is my color of choice, and the flowers, specifically, 'Lilies' are my favorite," She exclaimed in astonishment.

"I know because before you were born, I already knew you," the voice pleasantly whispered.

She reached for one of the flowers and plucked it from the ground and another one grew instantly in its place.

"This isn't possible," she claimed in wonderment.

"But, I assure you that all things are possible here," the small voice revealed.

"Do you know who I am?"

"Yes, sir. I do," Monica answered with certainty.

"You are God. The Holy One of all. The One within me," she continued answering as she smiled and emphasized, "You are my Savior."

The pleasant voice chuckled and responded, "I Am."

Suddenly, The Light flashed brightly as though someone had taken a photograph to seize the moment for the rest of all eternity.

"Monica," an illuminated being called out without making a sound from his mouth.

Monica opened her eyes as she became conscious of her surroundings.

She was flipped upside down on the passenger's side of Xavier's classic black Challenger still strapped securely in the seatbelt.

She looked over at Xavier, who appeared to be hurt pretty badly as the steering wheel was firmly pressed up against him crushing his chest.

"Monica?" The being repeated.

She turned in his direction and was greatly surprised.

"Who are you?"

The being smiled asking, "Would you ask me 'who am I,' instead of asking for my assistance?"

Monica didn't answer as the light coming from the spiritual being had entranced her.

He reached his arm out to give her a hand.

Monica smiled and obliged and immediately she was standing on the outside away from the car.

"You're an angel?"

"Surely, I am. I am an angel of The Lord," he answered without moving his mouth.

"What about my X-man?"

"Xavier's fine," he assured her.

"But, the car has flipped over and he is trapped inside

with shallow breathing," Monica said in a panic.

The angel of The Lord smiled gracefully as he looked at the old black car wrapped snugly around a Leyland Cypress tree.

"He'll be fine," the angel spoke into her mind.

Monica quickly turned around and was shocked to see that the car had miraculously flipped back right side up and Xavier was lying supine, comfortably outside of his vehicle on the grass.

She was amazed and couldn't pull away.

"Monica?" The angel called out to her again to redirect her attention back to him.

"God has a plan and He commanded me to see to it, that you and Xavier live. What the devil meant for evil, The Lord will use for good to bring glory to His name."

"Please, call for help," he urged, Xavier has a few broken ribs.

"You two will live, though," he said in a gentle loving voice before receding and vanishing from sight.

"Nine-one-one, state your emergency."

"My boyfriend and I have been involved in an accident."

As ambulance blared, Monica couldn't stop thinking about her experience in The Light.

It had caused a calm to consume her and she remained peaceful despite the circumstances.

She was calm although she knew in her mind that she should be freaking out.

Someone had deliberately ran them off the road and she had her suspicions as to who it was, but for now, she'd keep her mouth shut until she was sure.

"Ma'am, can you here my voice?" a paramedic asked as she shined a light in Monica's eyes.

"I can," she answered."

"What is your name and age?"

"I'm Monica Dupree and I am nineteen years old."

"Are you allergic to any medications, Monica?"

"I am not, but I am pregnant," she responded.

"How far along?"

"About eight weeks."

"The gentleman that's unresponsive, what is his name? Do you know if he's on any medications or if he's allergic to any?"

"His name is Xavier Shriver and he's seventeen. I'm not sure about his allergies. He has a sister that attends LCU with me. Her name is Letitia Shriver. You will have to contact her on campus," Monica responded before going unconscious.

"Why are you lying down there staring into space?" A female's voice asked as she softly giggled.

Monica cut her eyes to see a familiar face lying beside her with clasped hands propped under her chin wearing a luxurious smile.

"Who are you? I was told I'd survive. How'd I get back here?" Monica responded as she sat up and took a look around at the fuchsia lilies.

They were now accompanied with white ones and the

sky was night, but everything around them was clearly seeable as if it contained its own amount of light.

Monica could also clearly see galaxies in the sky as if they were huge paintings hung next to her.

"I'm just buying you some time," the familiar woman cheerfully answered.

"Time for what?"

"You'll find out soon."

"Why has the sky changed? How did these white lilies appear around each fuchsia lily in my field?"

The mysterious woman looked concerned for a moment before asking, "Do you know anyone who likes white lilies? Perhaps, they've put them around here. And what about space? Do you know someone who loves God's amazing creations in the heavens that are too far away for the human eyes to behold?"

Monica thought for a second and grew sad.

"My mom. She loved white lilies. My dad used to buy them every week for her and would add one single fuchsia lily in the middle of the bouquet for me."

"Well, I suppose they're from her," the woman replied and then asked, "What about space, who likes it?"

"My mom. She loved deep space. It fascinated her," Monica sadly responded, "she passed away almost six years ago.

"I'm sorry to hear that, but I believe life goes on after death and all passing truly is—is being transferred from one place to another," the woman confessed.

She sat up in the field and turned to Monica.

"If you knew for certain that heaven is real, do you believe that it would be specifically designed to our personal liking and preferences?" She asked Monica.

"I believe that's, indeed, so because otherwise it wouldn't be heaven to us," Monica truthfully answered.

"Well, could it be a possibility that this field is a part of your mother's heaven?"

Monica's eyes filled with tears as she thought long and hard about the probability that it could be very well so.

She looked up at the disguised woman as her familiar face became known to her.

"Mom," she exclaimed and embraced her as a waterfall of emotions came falling down around her.

"I come here often to think of you, Monica, my baby," Ramona revealed.

"I requested you meet me here to comfort and assure you that my death was not your fault," Ramona said as she cupped her hands around Monica's face.

"Besides, as you can see, I'm very much alive," she added grinning.

"Mom," Monica responded unable to form any other words as she couldn't believe it was really her.

"I am so proud of you, baby," she assured her.

"Can I stay here with you?"

"It isn't your time, sweetheart, furthermore, you're pregnant and will soon be married to an amazing young man," Ramona revealed.

"But, I've sinned against God and——."

"No, Monica. You're not outside of God's will. You were always destined to give birth to every particular child God has entrusted unto you, it's just that it'll happen sooner than intended which is no surprise to Him, dear," she answered her daughter before she could even completely get her sentence out.

"Come now. God has allowed me to show you something," Ramona told her as she stood up and grabbed her by the hand.

"You will be participating in this revelation, baby so brace yourself," Ramona warned.

Monica stood outside of her sons' bedroom eavesdropping on their bedtime story.

She began laughing as she listened to Xavier's account of Jesus being turned over to the Roman officials.

"Jesus was chillin' with twelve of his homies, and they called themselves, 'The Disciples, but at this point it was only like eleven of them because one of them wasn't quite disciplined and they were about to find out that their undisciplined boy, Judas, the twelfth one, was a trader—yo. Trader translated in the English language means, 'hater,' " she heard Xavier say as the twin boys laughed at their crazy dad.

"But, see it was one of them that was always, ' 'bout that drama,' though. His name was, Peter," he told them.

"Wow, same name like our grandpa?" The twin boys asked in unison and excitement.

"Yeah, exactly like your grandpa. Except, this Peter looked better," Xavier answered with brief snickering.

Monica shook her head and could barely hold back her laughter as Xavier told his interpretation of what happened next in the garden of Gethsemane.

"Anyway, one of 'The Twelve' was hating because Jesus was fly and his jealousy caused him to snitch. When they tried to jump Jesus, yo' boy Peter came out of nowhere and started blasting on them fools. He shot a dude's ear off and then oh boy was all like, 'Aaaah, my ear!' And, Jesus—."

Monica couldn't take anymore as she entered the bedroom to stop Xavier from telling his version of Judas's betrayal.

"Ok, X-man, that's enough. No more storytelling for you, love," she told Xavier cutting his Bible story short.

Xavier turned around to look at his beautiful wife and smiled as the boys whined, "No, mommy. Let dad finish telling what happened next. Pretty please."

Monica smiled and crossed her arms as Xavier winked at her then he turned back to face his sons and gave in to their plea for an ending.

"Jesus was all like, 'You have to forgive my boy, P. He be trippin' sometimes.' Then Jesus took this dude's ear and put it back on with His healing power," Xavier concluded.

The five year old boys looked up at their mom and asked, "Is that how it really happened, mom?"

Monica nodded slightly, "Yeah, almost. Let's go with that."

The twin boys were at awe, amazed by the story.

Xavier had been telling them a Bible story every night regarding the miracles that Jesus performed and the kids were amazed by them all.

"Whoa, Jesus was awesome," the boys exclaimed.

"Yes, and He still is," their parents agreed.

"Goodnight, Bryon and Byron—sleep tight, you two," Xavier softly said as he softly kissed them on their little foreheads.

"Xavier is going to be a great father and pastor."

"Wow, you really think so?" Monica asked surprised.

"Maybe, I know," she answered and winked.

"Twins?" Monica asked her mother in suspense.

"Twins," Ramona confirmed.

"Monica, you have to go back now. You were in surgery. There was bleeding on your brain. You've been in a coma for several days now, but it's time to wake up," Ramona revealed to her daughter as The Lord caused Monica to open her eyes.

15...A FUTURE AWAITS

"For I know the thoughts that I think toward you,

says the Lord, thoughts of peace and not of evil,

to give you a future and a hope."

-Jeremiah 29:11 (NKJV)

"When you don't have the courage to do it, in a dream,

I believe God shows you that you can when your body is

at rests and your spirit can walk and talk with Him.

There's something miraculous that happens inside of you

when you see yourself in a dream doing the very thing

you've convinced yourself you couldn't. It actually gives you the courage to do it because by God's power you've seen yourself doing it," Monica said to Xavier as she opened her eyes.

Xavier didn't understand what she was talking about because his only concern was her and he was beyond grateful that she had finally awakened.

I knew you'd wake up, Black Beauty," he said with hidden relief as he kissed her.

"I'm glad you're okay," she admitted concerning him.

"Of course, I am. You can't get rid of me that easily."

"I had the craziest dream," she revealed as she tried recalling it.

"What kind of dream?" Xavier asked Monica.

"It was about the accident."

Xavier looked puzzled as he thought about the accident and how it happened.

"But, it wasn't an accident."

"Of course it wasn't," Monica agreed.

"Why didn't you tell anyone?" Xavier asked.

"Because—."

"Uh oh, look who's awake," Monica's uncle, Patrick shouted as he entered her hospital room.

"You've had me stressed out for eight days."

Monica smiled at her uncle who she was more than happy to see, but grew agitated as he shares her father's face and she noticed that he hadn't been the first one to walk in her hospital room and discover she was awake.

She almost died and he didn't care enough to drive to Lubbock to see for himself that she'd survive, and stick around waiting and worrying if she'd wake up at all.

"Where's my dad? Did he come?" Monica asked hoping and praying to God that she was absolutely wrong about his absence.

"He had to leave, pumpkin," Patrick told her.

"He didn't even wait to see if I'd pull through."

"He did," her Uncle Patrick embellished.

"Then why isn't he here now?" Monica asked as she

dropped her head down and allowed tears to run down her cheeks.

"Of course, he didn't wait," she mumbled sadly under her breath.

"Monica, baby, he really wanted to stay, but Pamela called and said she wasn't feeling well and she begged him to come home. So, a few days ago when you started breathing again on your own, the doc took you off of the machine, and your blood pressure normalized, he decided to leave. He told me to tell you to call him once you were fully awake."

"Of course he went home to see about his wife," Monica said sarcastically.

"Aren't you tired of doing this, Uncle Patrick?" She curiously and exhaustedly asked him.

"Doing what?" He asked pretending as if he didn't have a clue what she was talking about.

"You know exactly what I'm talking about," Monica yelled.

"Are you yelling at me, Pumpkin are is it the hormones from this pregnancy?"

Monica didn't respond.

She lowered her head in shame.

"It'll be okay, beautiful," Xavier assured as he put his hand on her back.

"I know about the babies, Monica and you and I will be fine because as soon as you get well enough, I plan to marry you," Xavier revealed smiling.

"You gotta get well yourself, don't you?" Patrick asked Xavier frustrated.

"Besides, you're not even old enough to get married, kid," he reminded him, "we've already discussed this last night."

"And, like I told you last night, Mr. Dupree, I'll be eighteen before the babies are born," he reminded him.

"And besides, if Monica wanted to get married tomorrow we can. My mother wouldn't hesitate to sign a consent."

"Are you listening to yourself?" Patrick asked Xavier with a sincere demeanor.

"The fact that you've mentioned your mother in the same discussion regarding you getting married speaks clearly that you aren't ready."

The news was broken to Xavier more than a few days before by his devastated mother, Cassandra.

Xavier was talking to his sister, Letitia, who was the first person he saw upon awaking from surgery.

She had been worried sick about him and knew about the babies, but didn't want to terrify him with the news so soon.

Her plan was to wait until Monica comes out of her coma to tell him herself.

She thought that if Xavier found out too soon that Monica was in a coma and that she was pregnant, it would cause him more harm the necessary, considering he was already suffering from injuries that had the potential to be fatal.

Cassandra smiled when she saw Xavier was awake.

"Hey, baby. You had me worried sick about you. Don't ever do this again," she warned.

"I've been sitting with Monica's uncle, getting acquainted with him and watching the babies on the monitor."

Xavier's face went bleached-sheet white as his mother's words reached his ears.

"She's pregnant?"

Xavier turned to look at Letitia with fear-filled eyes.

"Tia, there's two of them?"

Letitia was horrified that her mother would break such news to her brother at such an awful time

"Mom! He didn't know that," Tia turned to her and shouted out in anger.

"He didn't know about one baby, and you've just told him about two babies, while he's still in a severely bad condition! Are you crazy? Are you trying to kill my brother?!" Tia scolded.

Cassandra looked at her daughter in contempt.

"Twins run in the girl's family, Tia. Monica's dad is a twin, and her dad's twin, has twins. He didn't know that? Surely, he should've tried getting to know her 'formally' before he decided to be 'informal' with her."

Cassandra turned to Xavier wearing disappointment.

"Xavier, baby, you're still in high school with a minimum wage paying job, and now you have not one baby on the way, but two babies on the way,"

Letitia's heart broke for her brother.

He stared in bewilderment and the vacant look in his eyes told her that he had completely tuned their mother out as his mind took a visit to another dimension.

"Mom, stop it for God's sake! What do you think you're doing? You're not helping him in any way whatsoever. You're only adding more fire, putting a lighter to a stove that's already lit."

Cassandra burst out in unbelievable laughter.

"Well, this stove is burning and there's two buns in the

oven," she sarcastically stated.

Letitia looked at her mother like she had lost her mind.

"Seriously? Are you serious, mom? That isn't funny, momma."

"It isn't a lie either," Cassandra snapped back.

"Now is not the time nor the place for this conversation. We're not arguing over something that's gonna happen, but something that has already happened, so what's the point?"

Cassandra's anger subsided as Letitia politely asked her to leave the room.

Letitia was ashamed that she didn't trust Xavier with the truth because of how she thought it would affect him.

She put her head down and quickly prayed to God in her heart for help to prepare Xavier's heart to receive the news regarding Monica even if it hurts beyond what he was able to bear.

"There was bleeding on her brain, Xavier," she began to calmly explain.

"During surgery to stop the bleeding, she slipped into a coma. She's on a machine to keep her and the babies alive until she's able to breathe again on her own. She kept this baby thing top secret and I really can't imagine how she's been dealing with it alone like this."

Letitia laughed as she thought about how much Monica always tend to overreact.

"When she wakes up and discovers that there's two babies wearing her, she's gonna go even nuttier than she already is."

Xavier, now more concern than ever for Monica, asked Letitia with tear-filled eyes, "Tia, sis, do you really believe she's gonna wake up?"

"Xavier, there isn't a single solitary doubt in my mind that Monica won't wake up."

Now, extremely concerned about his babies, he asked his sister, "What about our babies, Tia?"

Letitia smiled and provided reassurance to give Xavier hope for a lifetime.

"Brother, I've seen it; God showed me. I had a vision of you and Monica holding your sons."

Xavier smiled at Monica as he remembered and considered the day he found out about the babies.

He felt that, basically, Patrick thought of him as just another irresponsible kid.

He had just insulted him because he'd mentioned his mother would gladly sign a consent so they could wed.

Xavier had been arguing with Patrick all night about the situation with the babies and he was growing tired of his sly remarks regarding his age and the situation as if marriage wasn't an option because they were too young —especially him since he was, in fact, underage.

Their future is theirs to fight for, regardless and Xavier was willing to fight for the future that awaited them.

He stood up from the chair he was sitting in and held on to his chest to alleviate some of the pain from his broken ribs as he turned around to face her uncle with a few bible verses to backup his point.

"You mean like how the bible states, 'For this reason a man will leave his father and mother and be joined to his wife? No age was specified.' "

"But, you still aren't a man and in this situation it's called fornication, 'the act before marriage,' which means, you've both sinned against the very God that spoke those words. So in conclusion to your question, the scripture doesn't apply to this situation," Patrick remarked.

"Well here's a few that does, 'Have mercy upon me, Oh God, according to Your loving kindness. For I acknowledge my transgressions and my sin is always before me. Against You—and only You alone, Lord, have I sinned against,' " Xavier passionately expressed.

When Xavier had awakened and discovered that Monica was pregnant, he was shocked, but wasn't surprised.

He decided to do the right thing and ask Monica to marry him.

It wasn't like he didn't want to, anyway.

Monica means everything to him and as he came to the conclusion, he realized it would be an honor to be her husband and he knew she'd be honored to be his wife.

Xavier looked at Patrick with sincerity as he made the decision to come right out and say how he felt regardless if he found it disrespectful or not.

Patrick viewed him as just a kid and after dealing with his put-downs for a whole week, Xavier was done with his lack of respect for him because he was still in high school.

The truth is Monica's grown and is free to make her own decisions despite anyone's objection.

"And, Mr. Dupree, with all due respect, sir," Xavier began by respectfully saying.

"You may think that I'm still a kid and not yet a man, but as sure as I didn't miss, the results are proof that I am, indeed, exactly what you've said I'm not."

Patrick had to admit Xavier was brave for sticking up for himself.

He loved his niece like she was his own daughter.

He never told her that he always knew about her relationship with China.

He even knew why, but chose to let her make her own decisions only wanting, more than anything in the world, Monica to be happy.

Patrick could tell by the look in Monica's eyes that Xavier Shriver made her happy and it pleased him to see that he didn't lack courage and boldness.

He smiled in deep admiration and respect for Xavier, and then laughed.

He walked over, shook Xavier's hand, and commented truthfully, "I'm going to love having you around, son. I seriously like you."

Xavier was relieved as he smiled back at him and then turned around to wink at his future bride.

Monica smiled back at Him, and mouthed the words, "I love you, my X-man."

16...CAPTURED HEARTS

"You have captured my heart, my treasure, my bride. You hold it hostage
with one glance of your eyes."

—*Song of Solomon 4:9 (NLT, paraphrased)*

"Father God, in the name of Jesus, let the light of your
face shine down brightly on Your son, Xavier Eugène
Shriver and Your daughter, Monica Renee Shriver as
they start their new journey in the faith. Bless them, oh
Lord and their union. Guide them, my God in Your
truth, as they remain Yours, as they grow in You, and as

they grow in each other," Pastor Grant, Adrian's dad, prayed aloud as he placed one hand over Xavier's hands and chest, and the other in the middle of his back.

"And now, by the power given unto me from our Lord and Savior Jesus Christ, I now baptize you, Xavier Shriver, in the name of The Father, The Son, and The Holy Spirit."

As Pastor Grant pulled Xavier out of the water, he motioned for Monica to come forth to be baptized.

Monica's heart was beating up her ribcage as she stepped forward.

She had been baptized as a young child, but this time was different.

It was her choice and she was ready to give her whole heart to God and her husband.

"Take your shoes off, daughter of God. The place where you are standing is holy ground," she heard an elderly man's voice whisper from behind her.

Monica quickly turned around to see who was

whispering and was surprised to see that no one was there, but still, she obeyed and did what was asked of her.

Come on now, Monica. Don't be afraid," the pastor encouraged, "A new life for you and your husband, is about to begin.

"Monica pulled up her white robe a little above her ankles to avoid tripping as she entered into the crystal clear water in the baptistry.

She proceeded down the steps and allowed Pastor Grant to take her hand to aid in washing all of her sins away, and when he brings her back up, it'll be her new self that emerges, leaving her old self behind to drown to death.

"Are you ready for all things to become new, Monica?"

"I am, sir."

Do you accept Jesus Christ as your Lord and Savior?"

"I do, sir."

"Then, by the power given unto me from our Lord and Savior Jesus Christ, I now baptize you, Monica Shriver, in the name of The Father, The Son, and The Holy Spirit."

As Monica came up from the water, she became a new creature and she knew it because she felt it.

Old things had passed away, left buried in the true "watery grave."

This is what she wanted, and would fight to keep, always—peace, hope, and the greatest of all, Love.

Monica remembered her dreams, but hadn't shared them with anyone yet.

She knew she'd have twins and already knew their names, and also about the outcome of her marriage.

God had shared a beautiful thing with her and she'd seen, talked, and embraced her mother, but had seen other things too.

Monica started to remember and had discovered they were calling dreams.

God was calling her higher.

She'd seen herself in action, praying, laying hands on the sick, raising the dead, and casting out demons.

It was crazy and unbelievable at first, and just like she'd told Xavier the moment she awakened from her coma, "Sometimes you don't know you can do a thing until you see yourself doing it."

She was given by the Holy Spirit, the gift of faith and signs and wonders will follow her.

Seeing such a marvelous thing had awakened in her at the same time she had awakened from the coma.

"I know who I am now," Monica told Xavier the night she came home from the hospital.

"Then, who were you, before?" He asked joking.

"I'm serious, X-man." Monica told Xavier as she laid across his lap in Letitia's living room on the floor watching him play video games.

"Ok—ok. I'm sorry. Go ahead and say what you were about to say, bae."

"I know what God's plan is for me and I want to fully surrender my life to Him so His purpose for me can be fulfilled."

"Well, you're random," Xavier remarked grinning."

"I thought you said you'll be serious?"

"Oh, I did. I'm sorry."

"I didn't get a chance to finish telling you about what happened while I was in the coma, X."

"Dark Beauty, you did tell me, remember? You said you had a dream about our crash," he reminded her.

"That wasn't everything. Something else happened that was a part of another dream. I'm sure of it."

Xavier paused the game and turned his undivided attention to Monica.

"I want to be baptized."

"Okay, now. That's really random," Xavier responded confused more than surprised.

"You've never been baptized, Monica, and your father is a pastor?"

"When I was baptized at five years old it was because I was told to do so. I want to do it now by my own choice. God promised me in my coma that if I submit fully to

Him, He will use me. Our marriage will be blessed and our children will be blessed, as well," Monica began by explaining.

"X-man, he said to me, 'My people ask me to use them all the time, but very few want the change in themselves that must take place and is required to fully be used by Me. I desire to use you by working through you, not around you and in order for Me to work through you, I must change you.' "

Monica started tearing up as she recalled what The Lord had told her.

"He said, 'I don't just want you to see and hear about miracles and supernatural experiences, I want you to perform the miracles and experience the supernatural.' "

Xavier put his head down and took in a deep breath.

"I believe you," he confessed.

"I didn't want to sound crazy if I shared my dream, but after listening to you, I'm starting to think it wasn't just a dream," he admitted.

"In my dream, I was sitting in the grass under a tree. There was a gathering of people all around me waiting on this preacher to come share a word with us. When he made it to the platform, he kept repeating the same thing over and over, 'Repent and be baptized, every one of you, in the name of Jesus Christ for the forgiveness of sin and you will receive the Holy Spirit,' " Xavier explained.

"After a period of time, something started stirring up in me that made me want to go up there to preach the same. I stood up and walked up to the platform and without even asking, the preacher handed me the microphone and I began preaching the same message."

"Wow," Monica said.

She couldn't think of anything else to say.

Suddenly, she remembered what her mother said as they watched Xavier with the kids.

Ramona grinned and said, "He is going to be a great father and pastor."

"My God, X. That was a calling."

"Do you seriously think?" he asked, now considering it.

"Yeah, I really do," Monica answered as she came up with a brilliant idea.

"What do you say we have a double ceremony?"

"You mean, a wedding and a baptism?"

"No, A private wedding and a private baptism."

"If that's what you want to do, beautiful, then that's just what we'll do."

"Think about it this way—this will be a unique spin on two very sacred ceremonial events. We'll be making vows to our new life with Christ and our new life together."

"No objections here. Let's go ahead and elope."

"Why would you call it that?"

"Because, no matter how unique this spins, we're still running off in secret to get married."

Monica laughed, "Call it whatever you wish. This is going to be epic!"

"Right?! It's brilliant. I'll call Adrian's dad."

...And so, he did—and it was.

17...FORGIVING IS HARD

" 'Lord, how often will my brother sin against me, and I forgive him? As many as seven times?' Jesus said, 'I do not say to you seven times, But seventy-seven times.' "

—Matthew 18:21-22

"So, is it true? Did you really run off to get married because you're knocked up?"

"Seriously? The nerves! Why are you two even here? What is this an intervention or something?" Monica asked as she stood in her doorway.

"At church today, your dad asked for you because the

semester has ended and he knows your home, but not attending church. He sent me to check up on you and Dominique begged to tag along," Amberlee told Monica as her and Dominique stood outside on Monica's porch uninvited with a screen door between them.

"I'm only here to get some of my things. I've been in Dallas since the semester ended," Monica revealed.

"You still have a responsibility to let your family know what's going on and what you're up to," Amberlee said.

"This must be a joke," Monica responded and laughed.

"The nerves you have showing your face here with your kinship decrees of devotion after you and Kim tried to kill me and my husband. You have the potential to be a murderer, Amberlee, and Dominique, you're just an all out rapist. Now, get off of my porch before I call the cops and tell them everything that I know about y'all and have you arrested, and not just for trespassing."

Amberlee looked at Dominique in disgust wondering to herself what could Monica possibly mean by her accusation against him.

Monica smirked, folded her arms and leaned against the doorjamb.

"Oh, right. That's right. You never knew why I moved in with y'all, huh? Well, 'clueless cousin' let me give you a brief summary of an unfortunate event.

Monica looked upside Dominique's head and gave Amberlee a recap by truthfully stating, "Dominique had his way with me back when we were sixteen."

"He was my first. Do you remember, that beautiful night we shared together, stepbrother?" Monica asked with a great big overshadowing smile.

Dominique was mortified as he shamefully put his head down.

"But, he has repented and God has forgiven him. Ain't that right, Dominique?" Monica merrily teased.

"He has been redeemed and has gone out of his way ever since to make it up to Monica, but he had picked a bad day to tag along to her house.

She was highly suspicious and angry at Amberlee for a reason he clearly didn't know about.

Amberlee knew, though, that Monica suspected she was somehow involved in Kimberlee's attempt to run her and Xavier's car off the road with them in it.

"Monica, I've overdosed on remorse and the old me died three years ago as a result. I just wanted to make sure you are okay and figured you'd be more comfortable seeing me if I didn't come here alone," Dominique admitted.

"You raped my little cousin? You're a serious sex offender," Amberlee accused.

"You're no better, Amber, or have you forgotten?" Monica asked calmly as she opened the screen door and stepped out on the porch.

"I told my uncle Patrick about my suspicions of you and Kim's conspiring act against me. He don't wonna believe that you and her are capable of murder, but now that a seed of suspicion has been planted in his mind.

He'll stop at nothing to seek out the truth," she told her.

"You know him better than I do, Amber, so you know I'm right," Monica said as she kept walking closer to her cousin until she was only centimeters from the edge of the porch.

"Mark my words, Amberlee Dupree. The truth will come out—eventually."

Amberlee's eyes watered as she untruthfully confessed, "I'd never hurt you."

"But, you wouldn't necessarily stop your twin sister from doing so, though," Monica quickly responded with unclear emotions.

Nevertheless, Monica was right.

Amberlee wouldn't stop Kimberlee from doing any acts of evil, but she wasn't sure or not if she was capable of protecting her even unto someone's death.

She loved her twin sister and there's no in between whether her acts were good or bad.

Monica scoffed as she thought about how ridiculously

dysfunctional her family had been.

"My family is so awesome," she announced loudly and applauded in sarcasm.

"You go ahead and cover for her because you're no better than she is. I know what she's done and how you're covering it up. You have to live with that guilt, though, for the rest of your life. I don't want to see your lying stupid face again, Amber, because I know the truth and until you come out and admit it, I am not your little cousin. Now, get off my porch and off my property," Monica commanded.

Amberlee's face was scarlet as shame became her.

She wept as she stared sorrowfully at Monica and then at Dominique who was fully clothed in his very own tailor-made suit of opprobrium and contriteness.

She quickly turned away and rushed back to her car in anguish and drove off, leaving Dominique standing next to Monica.

"I guess that means I have to take you home?" Monica

asked Dominique as she looked over at him and took a deep breath.

"I can just call our dad if you like. He's been looking for an excuse to get over here, anyway," Dominique answered.

"No need. Stay here," Monica ordered as she went inside to grab her keys and purse.

She was beyond devoted to her family and didn't know why because they didn't deserve her devotion, but to her, forgiveness came easy as she unknowingly had the gift of mercy and was actively using it everyday without being aware of it.

As for Dominique, she hadn't actually accepted his friend request or anything, but she hadn't exactly blocked him either.

"When did you start wearing pants," Dominique curiously asked as he buckled his seatbelt.

"Around the same time I stop wearing short skirts," she smirk and answered with a sarcastic undertone.

"Guess I had that coming," he shamefully mumbled as they drove off.

They remained silent for the entire drive to their father's house as Dominique sulked in his mortification and Monica held on to her exhilaration.

She was happy now, and she wasn't going to allow anything from her past to take away that happiness she felt, or the love she'd found.

Dominique had come a long way and had found a genuine relationship with God.

Forgiveness is hard, but everyone must partake their portion in order to break free of bitterness and resentment.

Forgiveness is a healing process, but if you want a relationship with God, forgiving others are a spiritually mandatory requirement in order to be forgiven.

"What's good, Dominique?" Monica sincerely asked as they pulled up to their childhood home.

"I enlisted in the army," he revealed.

"Wow," Monica exclaimed.

"Right? Who would've thunk it." he said laughing.

It grew quite for a moment, almost to the point of being awkward.

"You're already showing," he said as he turned his attention to her baby bump.

"I know right?!" she agreed.

"May I?" Dominique politely asked in regards to touching her stomach.

"Sure, if you want to pull back a nub," Monica threatened with a straight face and exposed teeth.

Things were in a good place with them, but not that good.

"Right," Dominique said and quickly got out the car and went inside.

Monica took in a deep breath as she watched him enter the house.

She noticed her dad looking out of the window as she put her fuchsia BMW in reverse to drive off.

He ran outside to stop her.

"Sweetheart," he anxiously called out.

Monica put her car back in park and looked up at her father.

She lowered her head in defeat as he took a good look at her—his only daughter, who he missed dearly.

She looked up and locked eyes with him.

Neither one of them said a thing, but only stared for several minutes at each other.

Pamela and Dominique stood in the doorway watching them with pleasant smiles.

Tears filled her daddy's eyes as he continued to look at her who looked almost identical in likeness of her mother.

Monica sighed and got out of her custom-painted car.

She leaned up against the door and continued to allow him to see her.

"You're married?"

"I am, dad" she answered.

She crossed her arms as she grew emotional.

Her heart broke for him as she watched him break down in tears.

He thought he'd be the one who'd give her away one day, and he couldn't blame her for running off to get married, four years ago, he had ran off and did the same.

"Please don't cry, daddy," she politely asked as she fought back tears of her own.

"You're so beautiful and all grown up, Monica. I can't help it. You're married and I'm going to be a grandfather. And, you're wearing jeans, too, which actually looks quite nice on you," he admitted.

Monica gleamed as she broke out joyfully in tears.

"I'm going to be a grandfather," he repeated as he realized the depth of his statement.

"You're going to be a grandfather," Monica repeated and assured.

Pastor Dupree drew closer to his beautiful pregnant and newlywed daughter in jeans, and embraced her.

They allowed themselves to heal as they refused to let

go of each other.

No more words needed to be said, no more apologies, or no more blaming.

The bitterness and resentment had been exiled—an abandoned past, to start anew.

18...THIS IS IT

"And He said to her, 'Daughter, your faith has made you well.

Go in peace. Your suffering is over.' "

—Mark 5:34 (NLT)

"Xavier, it's time."

"Time for what?"

"Really? What else?"

"Monica?"

"Yeah, brother. Your wife is ready to give birth to my nephews. You and Adrian need to hurry up. She's having contractions back to back."

Xavier jumped to his feet in a panic as they all scurried around the house to get dress.

"This is it, Beauty. These boys are coming and they're coming fast," Xavier assured as he buckled her seatbelt.

But, all of that happened earlier, thirteen hours and forty-four minutes ago to be exact.

Monica, Xavier, Letitia, Adrian and Desirée was still waiting.

The babies, not even born yet, and already had a bizarre sense of humor.

They were running things from within the womb and their mom, dad, uncle, and aunts were exhausted.

Letitia and Desirée was lying in the hospital bed with Monica talking and waiting while the boys sat outside in the waiting room doing the same.

"You weren't going to call to tell anyone other than my dad, that you were admitted into the hospital and about to give birth to twins?" Amberlee scolded as she entered the room.

Monica gave her a look of pure disgust as she attempted to sit up in bed.

"Have you lost your mind, Amber?" Monica snapped.

"Amberlee, what are you doing here?" Desirée asked as she tried picking up on her emotional and spiritual state.

"She must be lost," Letitia turned and told them.

"You have some nerves coming here uninvited and if I wasn't connected to all this stuff and could get up, I'd slap you around in Jesus' name."

Amberlee put her head down in shame and took a deep breath.

"I deserve that," she sadly admitted.

"Well, I can get up," Letitia told her fully prepared to fight if it became necessary.

"So, you better quickly move around," she threatened.

"Wait a sec, Monica and Tia," Desirée insisted.

"Something's wrong," she told them.

She had picked up on Amberlee's emotions and

became overwhelmed with the weight of her sorrow.

"Do you feel justified, Amberlee?" Desirée asked as God revealed her reason for being there.

"No, but how do—?"

"But, you want to?" Desirée asked cutting her off.

Amberlee lowered her head as tears dropped from her face onto the white marble hospital floor.

She was ashamed and filled with remorse.

Amberlee looked up at Monica with fear and regret in her eyes, but was determined to make things right again with her favorite little cousin.

"I just rode two and a half hours from Copperas Cove with my dad because I needed to see you, Monica."

Monica face hadn't soften one bit and still held the appearance that shared with everyone in the room that she was furious, but she loved Amberlee and even in her anger she wanted to hear what she had to say.

"So, where's my uncle?"

"Out front, giving us time to talk."

"Well, hurry up and say what it is you have to say, so you can get out of my room and my uncle can come in."

She really didn't want to be mean to Amberlee, but every time she open her mouth, words just kept coming out rudely.

Amberlee took in a deep breath before coming clean and completely confessed to the accusation against her and her twin.

"I turned in Kim, Monica," she revealed, "Because, what was done to scare you, almost killed you, my two little baby cousins, and a man that had nothing to do with our family quarrel"

"When my dad came to me and asked me about the car crash, he had already went to her first, but she lied about everything. When he kept pressing the issue, she became angry and told him that you got what you deserved, but of course he didn't have any evidence to go to the police, so I gave it to him."

"Why did you, Amber?" Monica asked as her face

began to soften.

"Because, like I said before, the intent was to scare you, not run you all off the road or try to kill you. I've always known what Kim was capable of, Monica, but you have to believe me, trying to make y'all crash was never my own intentions."

Monica was confused and really wanted to believe her.

She looked over at Desirée for reassurance, with the full knowledge of knowing if anyone knew for sure that Amberlee was telling the truth, it would be her.

"She's telling the truth, Monica," Desirée reassured.

Monica's nerves relaxed as she flashed a smile at her favorite cousin, Amberlee, and motioned for her to come closer and give her a hug.

Something felt strange, though.

The pressure in her stomach that was so tight before, loosened and she immediately felt better.

"Eww, gross! This is not cool, Monica! Did you just pee in the bed? That's what the bedpan is for," Letitia yelled with a disgusted look on her face.

Desirée quickly jumped up out of bed in a panic and snatched the covers back off Monica.

"Tia, you have to get the guys. Amberlee, go out front to get the nurse and Dr. Whitaker. Also, tell your dad. Let them know that Monica's water just broke."

"Oh my God," Monica exclaimed, "This is it, they're coming."

Amberlee quickly ran back inside with three nurses who quickly got to working on Monica and preparing the room for the procedure.

Amberlee rushed over to Monica's side, grabbed her hand, and began to imitate long in and out breaths instructing Monica to follow.

"I get to finally use my skills. I wonder if I can get this time counted towards my internship," she joked causing the girls to laugh.

"You're going to make an amazing doctor someday, Amber," Monica complemented.

"I'm here, Beauty," Xavier said rushing to her side while her uncle and Adrian stood at the door afraid to enter the room.

"Hey, pumpkin. You can do this. I'm just gonna hang tight out here with my boy—what's your name again?" Patrick asked.

"Adrian."

"Yeah, Adrian and I are gonna just hang around out here to allow y'all handle y'all's business."

"Well, can I get you two 'Bravehearts' to step aside so I can get these twins out here with us," Dr. Whitaker said grinning as he entered the room.

"All set, doctor," one of the nurses announced as they completed the preparations to deliver the boys.

"Deep breaths in and out, Mrs. Shriver. You're doing great," the nurses coached.

Then all of a sudden, Xavier and Monica's whole lives changed forever as their sons were properly introduced.

"Hello, boys. Welcome to the world."

EPILOGUE

"I am dark, but I am beautiful."

—Songs Of Solomon (NLT, paraphrased)

Monica stood in front of her full-length mirror holding up an elegant V-neck casual evening dress against her curves that was a beautiful shade of fuchsia.

Her husband had bought it and he'd asked her to wear it this night along with a pair of princess cut diamond earrings.

She had been devoting the majority of her time to the

boys, but tonight was her night and she had plans with her X-man downtown for a festive evening of dancing and fun to enjoy each other as one.

It was the first weekend they've had alone since the twins arrived and they were overly excited when her uncle, Patrick and favorite cousin, Amberlee called offering to keep the kids for a few days to give them some time to care for themselves by spending quality time with each other.

Monica had decided to move to Dallas, but would still keep her country house in Copperas Cove as a second home for their family whenever they felt like getting away.

Xavier and Monica were in love with their new loft that just so happens to be right across the way from the other newlyweds, Adrian and Letitia Grant that had recently broken the news that they're going to have a baby girl soon.

Desirée and Chase's relationship was getting pretty serious as every time you saw one of them, the other you'd see also.

The future was looking promising for them.

Xavier decided not to waste any time waiting to enroll in college and his mother and stepfather, along with Monica's uncle, dad, and stepmother, are all on board to pitch in with helping raise the twins until their young and in love college parents graduate.

For that is why having a supportive family and friends are so important because as we work together, helping and depending on one another, a fulfilling and rewarding life is formed for all of us.

Indeed, they're married students with kids, but are making their lives together, work—with God and no regrets.

This way of living life may be impossible for most, but they've chosen to be the example that it can surely be done.

Perfectly within the will of God, of course, but the norm was never meant for them.

As Monica put on her makeup and got dress, she thought over her life.

She could've remain a sullen soul living the rest of her life brooding over what life has done to her until she die, but she realized we're given this amazing experience called life.

Unfortunately, this amazing gift of life comes with the good and the bad; continue living and you are sure to experience them both before you die.

All life is—is living, but all those living life aren't alive.

To live life abundantly, is to be alive—after all, isn't that why Jesus came?

So a question is posed: Are you alive living your life, or just living your life until you die?

Monica thought on these things as she sat peacefully waiting downtown in Dallas surrounded by the city lights while her husband, Xavier paid for valet parking and checked on their reservations.

As she leaned back and crossed her legs, she looked up

and caught a glimpse of her reflection in the tinted glass panel of a building across from where she was sitting.

Monica suddenly came to the conclusion that she wasn't just living, but is very much alive and living life abundantly, just as God intended.

Every experience, good and bad, were all worth living through and if it wasn't for the bad times, there'd be no appreciation for the good ones.

Being alive and in the moment, she appreciated.

Monica considered her dark skin that's neither good nor bad, but simply beautiful because of a diverse God.

With a pleasant mien, she softly prayed in a whisper,

"I love you so much, Lord. I'm beautiful dark—just the way You created me, so thank You for my life. I am so blessed to be alive." **—Never End**

BEFORE YOU GO

I hope you enjoyed this book. If so, please be so kind to rate it on Amazon.com and give a review. Also, follow me on Twitter and, or like my page on Facebook @WriteousSeries for updates and new releases. You can also stay connected with me and subscribe to my blog at WriteousAuthor.com Thanks so much for reading...remain blessed.

OTHER BOOKS BY AUTHOR

Writeousness: Tia's Pursuit

(The Writeous Series, Book One)

"Her eloquent writings and constant pursuit serve as proof—she believes God, and therefore her faith is accounted for righteousness."

Psalmissiveness: Tia's Purpose

(The Writeous Series, Book Two)

"By eloquent writings from the book of Psalms, Tia submits to God's perfect plan for her life."